C000148581

Benno Massimo had treated Tania abominably—but his stern brother Vicente chose to believe that the boot was on the other foot and that Tania was responsible; and when Benno died he blamed her for that too. So how was it that not much later she found herself blackmailed into marrying him?

Books you will enjoy
by JANE ARBOR

ONE BRIEF SWEET HOUR

Lauren's Caribbean holiday was meant to be a
once-in-a-lifetime thing, the end of her un-
happy life and the beginning of a new one. So
the last thing she wanted was to run into the
unhappiest part of that past life: Dale Ransome.
And if Dale chose to think the worst of her, let
him. She just didn't care any more—did she?

WHERE THE WOLF LEADS

'Where the wolf leads, the pack will follow,'
Dracon Leloupblanc said arrogantly—and
where he was concerned it certainly seemed to
be true. But in his case everyone seemed to
behave like sheep rather than wolves. And
why, thought Tara Dryden indignantly,
should she add herself to their number?

THE DEVIL DRIVES

Una hadn't doubted Zante Diomed's love for
her any more than she had doubted her own
for him—so it was a dreadful shock when she
learned that he had married her for one reason:
revenge. How could she prove to him how
wrong he was—and in her despair and disillusion, did she even want to now?

PACT WITHOUT DESIRE

When Cliff Iden jilted her to marry another
girl, Sara declared she would marry the first
man who asked her, just to 'show' him—which
was why she had rashly accepted Rede
Forrest's proposal. But she hadn't anticipated
that Rede would take her out to Singapore, to
be constantly thrown into the company of Cliff
and his new wife. Nor had she anticipated all
the other emotional problems that would arise
so unexpectedly . . .

INVISIBLE WIFE

BY

JANE ARBOR

MILLS & BOON LIMITED
15–16 BROOK'S MEWS
LONDON W1A 1DR

*All the characters in this book have no existence out-
side the imagination of the Author, and have no relation whatsoever to anyone bearing the same name or
names. They are not even distantly inspired by any
individual known or unknown to the Author, and all
the incidents are pure invention.*

*The text of this publication or any part thereof may
not be reproduced or transmitted in any form or by
any means, electronic or mechanical, including photo-
copying, recording, storage in an information retrieval
system, or other, without the written permission of the
publisher.*

*This book is sold subject to the condition that it shall
not, by way of trade or otherwise, be lent, resold, hired
out or otherwise circulated without the prior consent
of the publisher in any form of binding or cover other
than that in which it is published and without a similar
condition including this condition being imposed on the
subsequent purchaser.*

First published 1981
Australian copyright 1981
Philippine copyright 1981
This edition 1981

© Jane Arbor 1981

ISBN 0 263 73533 8

Set in Monophoto Plantin 11 on 12 pt

*Made and printed in Great Britain by
Richard Clay (The Chaucer Press) Ltd,
Bungay, Suffolk*

CHAPTER ONE

STIFF-LIMBED, moving like a robot, Tania went
to the luggage cupboard adjoining her room and
took from it the leather-strapped canvas holdall
which had carried at least half of her personal
wardrobe when she had come out to Italy from
England.

In the cupboard too was the set of cream pig-
skin valises she had acquired since, but with a
shiver of recoil she shut the door upon it. The
holdall and her shoulder-bag must suffice for all
she would be taking with her when she left the
Villa Massimo. Soon now and on foot, and she
wouldn't be coming back . . .

The evening had darkened too early; thunder
was rolling in the distance, and she couldn't let it
matter that it was beginning to rain, for she
needed the dark for her escape. But a couple of
hours ago the windows of the Villa's *salotto* had
been curtained against the late afternoon sun; the
elegant room had been dim when she had stood
in its doorway, momentarily allowing her eyes to
focus to the half-gloom before going in.

She had been on her way into the garden,
stopping in the hall to call her hairdresser in
Venice, only to see that the telephone was not in
its niche. She had had to follow the clue of its

extension cord to the door of the *salotto*, and when she could see more clearly she had made out Benno in tennis shorts and shirt, jack-knifed across an easy chair with its high back to her. His legs dangled over its arm and the telephone was cradled in the V which his posture made between his thighs and his body.

He was so still that she thought he had fallen asleep. But when she was about to tiptoe across to surprise him with an English 'Bo!' she had noticed he had the receiver to his ear and was listening.

She had turned to leave when his sudden laugh halted her and his seductive Italian voice questioned, 'What do you mean—what about Sophia; is it still "on" between us? My dear fellow, Sophia Greniere and I are a permanency; I'm reckoning on no problem there, except her insane jealousy. But she must know there is no way I'd allow a bagatelle like marriage to my young nonentity to come between us. Naturally Sophia doesn't like it, but there was this wide-eyed, straw-coloured orphan sitting on a potential goldmine in this *horror* of an English Midland town—indeed, Pascale, you cannot imagine how drear!—and if I'm to keep Sophia in the state she expects, it was too good a chance to miss. . . . What's that?'

He had listened again briefly. Tania had waited, too shocked to feel shame at her eavesdropping. Then: 'Couldn't I have bid for the goldmine and left the maiden sitting? Difficult that, without the hard cash to offer, and you know Vicente. He wouldn't gamble ten lire on something he hasn't vetted for himself. So it seemed simpler and cheaper to marry the waif into the family and get the scheme, whatever its worth to us, for nothing.'

Benno had paused there, then had mused, 'Mind you, I had to force myself. She, Tania—Tania Morre, English on her mother's side, but speaking Italian like one of us, both parents dead—had got in touch with us in the first place, and Vicente sent me to England to see her. After that I went twice more, and finally brought her back, engaged to me. At first she was as frigid as a bite into an unripe apple. But she melted under my well-known charm; Madrigna approves, thinking I shall "settle down". Vicente, as always, keeps his counsel, and we are to be married next week. If you hadn't been half across the world, I'd have kept you posted on the affair. But you will be around now for some time, and we can meet?'

There was another pause, during which the man named Pascale must have spoken. But Benno said next, 'No, not tonight. I have a date with Sophia. Another time? I'll be in touch——'

He had returned the receiver to its rest, and Tania had fled, scrambling blindly up the marble staircase to her room. Locking its door—as if that were any safeguard against a world gone cruelly awry—she had looked at its tasteful luxury of cool, cream walls, graceful tapestry chairs, satin-draped windows and the large embroidered 'M' which appeared on every bedhead in the main rooms of the Villa Massimo.

She had been made welcome to it and to the Villa by Benno's widowed stepmother, Signora Fabia Massimo, and when she had found herself alone in it for the first time, she had whimsically traced with her finger the scrolls of that 'M', soon to belong to her, and she had tested aloud the sound of 'Tania Massimo', in place of the 'Tania Morre' to which she had been born, twenty-one years ago.

And now, by reason of Benno's crude, cynical revelations to his unseen friend, the room belonged to her no longer, nor she to it. Any more than did the trousseau she had collected lovingly; any more than did her promised future as Benno's wife . . .

For a long time she had remained sitting in the chair by the window looking out over the garden slopes to the Brenta, the river which wound its sluggish way between Padua and Venice, and whose banks had housed the palatial homes of the rich of both cities over the centuries. Some of the villas were now derelict, some were show places for tourists, other were private schools, and others still, comparatively modern, had their swimming-pools and tennis courts and yachts on the river and were mostly owned by the masterminds of the cities' business interests—the tourism, the leather craft, the shipping, the lace, the glass, immemorially famous.

One such house was the Villa Massimo, but tonight Tania's view of its lawns and flowers and river frontage was curtained by rain, and even if it had not been, her gaze would have been unseeing while her thoughts jostled for place in her understanding of what had just happened to her.

She could have made a mechanical exercise of dictating Benno's talk, word for betraying word, for the benefit of anyone who couldn't know where the particular daggers stabbed. For instance—'*This wide-eyed, straw-coloured orphan*'. At the remembered humiliation of that wound she consciously used her eyes to ask of the long mirror across the room how much or how little she deserved its thrust.

Straw-coloured. Yes, her mother's English fairness of hair had come to her in pale tints well this side of gold, but not, surely, the dirty grey-yellow of straw, and its brushed length shone as the brittleness of straw never could. And wide-eyed? Benno's belittling judgment had made of her eyes two glassy marbles. True, they were pale grey, fringed by gold lashes and large by contrast with her other features of small straight nose, short upper lip and narrowing chin. But they weren't the bulbous orbs of Benno's scorn. Though, since puzzlingly he saw her only as a potential moneybag, probably he hadn't noticed that they could darken and crinkle and laugh. Any more than, for all his skilled courtship of her, he had cared that she was slim and woman-shaped, so long as she had melted flatteringly to his charm.

And where had it all begun?

She hadn't known of his existence when, keep-

ing her promise to her dying father, she had written to the Massimo family at an address no more
definite than *Crystos*, *Venice*, because he had said
it couldn't fail to find one of the most notable
crystal-makers of the crystal-fashioning city. Nor
had it failed.

The typewritten reply had been signed by one
Vicente Massimo, who explained that he was now
head of the firm; he and his younger brother
Benno were the fifth generation of Massimos in
Venetian glass. It was news to him that Reggio
Morre had a daughter. His only knowledge of the
Morre family was that Reggio's father had been a
valued employee of his, Vicente's, own grandfather, when he had broken with Crystos after
marrying an Englishwoman and had gone to set
up a glass foundry of his own in England. But in
view of Tania's letter, Vicente's brother, who
would presently be in England on Crystos business, would call upon her to condole with her on
her father's death.

And so handsome, debonair Benno had 'called',
bringing a breath of Italian warmth to a bleak
English spring. Over the telephone he had been
unjust to Norbridge, the prosperous little industrial town nestling under the Malvern Hills. But
Tania had been ashamed of the evidence of her
father's failure which she had had to show him—
the closed foundry behind the house which she
had been about to put on the market before finding herself a job.

The oven fires were dead, the crucibles empty,

the sales showroom which had been her own province filled only with packing-cases of items which had not found buyers in the closing-down sale. But Benno, looking at the sorry wreck, had been sympathetic, and in her efforts to be loyal to her father she had repeated all his excuses for having let down his own father's enterprise.

The small man couldn't compete with the 'big men's' monopoly of the industry; he had no capital with which to develop his ideas; no one was interested in helping him. Tania had heard it all so often that she told it to Benno like a well-learned lesson. And though Benno had listened and questioned and had helped with the sale of her house and with Reggio's business papers, she had not understood at all his reference to a 'goldmine' for which he claimed to have asked her to marry him. If her father had had any lucrative plans for the future, they had died with him. He had not confided them to her. But in dealing with Reggio's affairs, was it possible Benno had read into them some possibilities which, since he had not mentioned them to her, he was keeping to himself? From his confident boast to his friend, she supposed it must be so. But it was something she would never know now . . .

Romance had blossomed from Benno's solicitude and from her own loneliness. He was the most personable man she had ever met. He had persuaded her to spend some of the proceeds of her house sale on clothes and cosmetics; had discouraged her efforts to look for a job, and on his third visit, when he had taken her into his arms there was a new intensity, an infectious heat to his lovemaking which had melted her resistance to the idea of marrying him after so short a courtship.

And so, innocent and trusting and in love with love, she had come to the Villa Massimo to be married from Benno's home. Fabia Massimo, whose elegance had come to terms with middle age, had welcomed her as a fiancée for Benno of whom she approved. About her elder stepson's welcome Tania had never yet been sure.

Vicente Massimo was a dark enigma, his own contained man who gave nothing of himself away, but claimed and took with harsh authority, brooked no fools, found no excuse for weakness. Thwarted, he might even turn physically cruel— Such was her judgment of his character, borne out by the daunting arrogance of his looks and manner.

Feature by feature, his eyes were black beneath heavy lids, his dark hair sleekly styled to a curve at his nape—in three months Tania had never seen it ruffled. His nose was proudly Roman, high-bridged with flared nostrils; the spare, bronzed flesh of his face was tightly drawn over cheekbones and square obstinate jaw. There was hauteur to the lift of his chin and his tall body was a pillar of mature virility, its owner very sure of its power. Only his full-lipped sensual mouth spoke to the Latin blood in his veins. All else about him seemed carved in granite.

His manner with Tania was distant. She thought he had no more natural curiosity about her than a feudal lord might have about a female serf, though more than once she had caught him studying her, as if to register some private impression of her, at which he meant no one else to guess. Sometimes, baffled by his iron control, she wondered what experience or emotion would rouse him to unbridled passion—if anything could. She shuddered for the woman who would marry his mastery, his dominance. Shuddered—but wondered what life with him would be like . . .

It was full evening now, time for her to go. Fabia Massimo was out, she knew. Vicente did not usually come back from his Venice offices until dinner-time, and, relieved but not surprised that Benno hadn't sought her out before going to his rendezvous with his mistress, she had heard him go his room earlier and leave again. She must write her letter to him, the only notice of her leaving she meant to give.

While she wrote, sparing him none of the bitterness which consumed her, she realised that she could not have turned against him so abruptly if she had ever loved him. Love would have excused him, needed to hope, blinded her into marrying him, notwithstanding. At least she was escaping that.

She took the letter to his room, propped it in full sight on his bureau and returned to do her packing, which took longer than she expected. It was more than half an hour later when she pulled the hood of her raincoat over her head, took a last look round the room and closed its door.

She reached the stairs head, only to freeze at the sound of someone coming up from around the curve of the stairs. Who? One of the maids? No, they used the back flight. Fabia? Vicente? Benno himself?—oh *no*! One hand on the balusters, the other clutching the long holdall, Tania waited as Vicente mounted towards her, pausing to stare at her from the last stair but one.

She stared back dumbly, knowing his scrutiny had taken stock of her luggage and her rainwear. He took the last stair and stood level with her, looking not up at her now, but down. He said with a suavity which did not deceive her, 'You are going out? In this deluge? Benno is driving you?'

She shook her head. 'No.'

'No?' He waited.

Her throat constricted. 'No,' she echoed, her voice rough. 'I'm not just on my way out anywhere. I'm—leaving.'

If her intention had really deceived him she would have expected an incredulous '*Leaving*?' from him. But after a moment's silence he merely said in a tone which splintered with ice, 'I—see. I am your host, you are engaged to my brother, our stepmother has welcomed you as her future daughter. But finding yourself unsuited here, you are leaving for somewhere else. Would it be too impertinent to enquire where?'

'For nowhere in particular. Just away,' she

muttered lamely, and ventured a step forward, only to find his hand clamped about her free wrist. It was the action of a captor, but his voice was still sarcastically polite.

'Then if not your destination, your reasons, perhaps?'

She had to answer something, but since Benno, in all justice, must be the first to learn her reasons, she evaded with, 'I've found I don't love Benno enough to marry him.'

'Indeed? A sudden decision, isn't it? Have you told him so?'

'No, he is out. I have left a letter for him in his room.'

Vicente's black eyes snapped. 'The classic runaway ploy! As a prize coward you run true to type. How were you proposing to travel?'

She did not like the sound of 'were you'—as if he thought he could stop her. 'I shall walk to a garage at Mestre and hire a cab.'

'To take you where?' he asked again.

Tania compressed her lips, and when he saw she did not mean to reply, he reached for the holdall, giving a sharp rap to her knuckles when she clung to its handle. 'This can go back to your room, because you are not leaving this house until you have seen Benno,' he said. Passing her, he took the holdall to her room and came back to the stairhead. 'Meanwhile, this letter——' Leaving her standing, he went down the corridor to Benno's room, went in and returned to her.

In a dangerously quiet voice he said, 'So—a liar

as well as a cheat! You left no letter there for Benno.'

Tania stared. 'I *did*! On his bureau where he couldn't miss it.'

'It's not there now. Look for yourself.'

She did. He was right. Her letter had gone, and the only explanation could be that Benno had returned after first going out and now had it with him. When she rejoined him, she said as much to Vicente, who scorned, 'He found and read a letter like that without troubling to find out what you meant by it—that takes some believing, don't you think?'

The injustice of his doubt enraged her. 'You don't take my word that I wrote to him?' she demanded.

'Frankly, no. That shouldn't surprise you. Not that it matters either way now, since you are coming down to the *salotto* with me to wait until Benno comes home, when, face to face with him, you will—talk. Come.' He went ahead of her down the stairs.

Following him to the door of the *salotto*, she turned on him, choking impotently, 'You can't keep me against my will!' But she didn't doubt that he could when, without replying, he went on into the room, pointed to a chair and ordered her, 'Sit down.'

Tania remained standing where she was, hands in the pockets of her raincoat, resisting him when he tried to draw it off her shoulders. Abandoning the effort, Vicente went to sit down himself, remarking, 'I believe Madrigna is dining out, so if we have to wait long for Benno, we may have to dine tête-à-tête—do you mind?'

She clenched her teeth. 'I'm not going to eat with you, please don't think it!' she defied him.

'Nor sit either in the company of your warder?' he insinuated. At which, hating his return to suavity even more than his implied threats, she moved to a chair as far from him as possible and sat down, defeated and, seeing herself for the first time as the cowardly runaway he thought her, was shocked by the intensity with which she cared that he should doubt her good faith.

He was nothing to her, and would be less once she had left the Villa Massimo behind her. And yet supposing she told him of Benno's heartless betrayal which had driven her to her panic flight, would he soften a little, understand her revulsion, forgive?

Almost tempted, she looked across at the impenetrable mask of his face, and remembered in time that admission of his trickery of her was Benno's right. She mustn't whine to Vicente before he made it.

Into the charged silence the sound of the telephone came almost as a relief.

'Excuse me.' Vicente went to answer it, but brought it back on its cord, as if he did not trust Tania not to escape while he was engaged with it.

'Yes, speaking.' He said nothing more for some minutes, then sharply, 'When was this? How badly? Yes . . . Yes, I understand. Yes, I can be there—' he glanced at his watch, 'in fifteen minutes.' He replaced the receiver and looked across at Tania.

'That was the police,' he said. 'Benno has had a car accident. Rushed the level crossing beyond Mestre to beat the Milan–Venice express, was caught and dragged by the engine until the train could be stopped. It took some time to extricate the car, which was a mere bundle of metal; Benno was unconscious when they pulled him free, and still was when they sent him to hospital——'

'Oh—h!' Tania stifled her long cry of shock with a hand over her mouth. She was shaking as if with an ague, and when she tried to stand the room spun and she sank back again. Vicente came over to her. 'Easy,' he said, and thrust her head down between her knees, leaving her so to bring the blood back into her head while he went to the drinks cabinet and poured a cognac. At her side again, he put a hand on her shoulder. 'Drink this,' he ordered, and she sat up, her eyes swimming.

'I—I can't,' she shuddered.

'*Drink it!*' He held the glass to her lips as if it were a feeding-cup, tilting it to her sips until she had drained it empty.

He put it aside. 'I have to go. The police want me there.' He paused, studying her. 'Can I leave you?' he asked.

She flinched. 'You mean—can you trust me not to escape?'

'If that's how you read me.'

'I think that was what you meant. But couldn't I come with you—please?'

He said impatiently, 'If you see it as your belated duty, very well. I haven't time to argue with you. I'll fetch my car. Be at the door when I bring it round.'

The scene at the level crossing was an eerie one of shifting crowds and neon lights and shadow-casting lanterns. Camera bulbs flashed whitely and passengers from the held-up express queued for the buses which would take them on to the Venice railway station and the water-taxis for the city. A knot of police was gathered round the wreck of the car. The man who came to open the door of Vicente's car looked in at Tania as Vicente alighted.

'The *signora*?' he questioned.

'The car driver's fiancée,' Vicente said shortly. 'She will stay here.'

Tania watched as he joined the group to become the recipient of the gestured explanations as to how the collision had happened. He listened, questioned out of her hearing, and reached into what remained of the car's driving seat to take something from it before he returned to his own car, pursued by reporters.

He shut the door on them and waved them away. A minute or two later he was speeding to-wards Venice.

'Where now?' Tania asked, though she could guess.

'The hospital for me. I shall put you into a taxi

on Piazzale Roma, to go back to the Villa to wait for Madrigna until she comes in, and if I am not back myself, you will tell her.'

Tania dipped her head obediently. 'All I know,' she agreed. 'But how could it have happened?'

'The police have witnesses to his mad speeding before he reached the crossing, and he rushed through the barrier just as it was closing. The far barrier had come down before he reached it, and the train hit the car broadside on at a hundred and twenty kilometres an hour.'

He was in a hurry to keep his date after he had returned home for something and had found her letter, thought Tania, as Vicente went on, 'One of the men who will give evidence at the enquiry is going to swear that in his view the car driver seemed intent on suicide.' Vicente paused. 'Does that say anything to you?'

Tania drew a long shuddering breath. 'Suicide? *No*! Why should it?'

They had reached the wide *campo* of Piazzale Roma and he slid the car into a parking slot before taking something from his pocket and passing it to her. 'Then perhaps this will?' he said.

She stared at the crumpled paper he had put into her hand. It was the torn half of an evelope with the letters, 'Ben——' above a broken underlining in her handwriting. She cupped it open. There was nothing inside it, but it had been there in the car—proof which she could offer to the doubter beside her.

She said, 'My letter to Benno. You didn't believe I wrote it, did you?'

Vicente said, 'No. But don't look for apologies, please.'

'I don't——'

'Just as well, since my finding the thing damns your case even worse than if you had, as I thought, skulked off without a word of explanation of your going——'

Tania broke in, '*Damns*?' she faltered.

'For want of a stronger word, yes. For you did write your letter, breaking with Benno without giving him a hearing. He did get it and read it— and what was the result? Instead of wanting or trying to see you to confront you with it—as I'd have done, if only to ram it piecemeal down your throat—he drives off in a fury of need to put distance between you and him until his sanity can take in the fact of his being jilted without cause practically on the eve of his wedding. So he drives like a madman, like a fool for love, like a—near-suicide. And *now* do you understand "damns"?'

Tania shrank in her seat. She had wondered what this man might be like in anger, and now she knew. By the intermittent light of the cars which jockeyed for parking space about them, his black eyes seemed to blaze with a red fire, sparking and shadowing in turn, and his rabid virulence was all for her. She said faintly, 'I *had* cause. I didn't love him.'

'Hm—you could have fooled me. And apparently, over three months of a halcyon engagement, you did fool Benno to the point of what you sprung on him tonight—I hope to your lasting shame. Or is that too much sense of guilt to look for from a taker like you?'

That was too cruel. She must defend herself. 'I'm *not* guilty of what happened to Benno tonight,' she protested. 'He *wasn't* speeding desperately because of me. He was——' But there the words she had planned should follow froze on her lips. (*He was late. He was going to meet his mistress, and he had tricked me into our engagement for some greed of his own.*) She mustn't say them until Benno was in a position to admit they were the truth, as he would have to, once he recovered. She said instead, 'He must have been late for wherever he was going, and you know how fast he drives even normally.'

'Fast, but not recklessly. No, there has to have been a cause, and on the evidence we've found, I'd say we know it.' Vicente opened his door and stepped out. 'Stay where you are until I bring a taxi for you. And remember—for Madrigna's hearing tonight, you did not write Benno a letter, I did not catch you on the point of flight, we were together in the *salotto* when the police telephoned, and naturally, as Benno's fiancée, you wanted to go with me to the crash. You understand?'

'Ye-s, but——'

'But what?' he rasped impatiently.

'You're asking me to act a lie.'

'While Madrigna has one shock to take, yes. And anyway, until you suddenly decided to cut loose, while you have pretended to be happy with

Benno for the past three months, haven't you been lying to us all?' He shut the car door with a bang and strode away.

Before they had left the Villa Vicente had given the bare news to Maria, Fabia Massimo's housekeeper, and when Tania had returned she had told the woman the little more that she knew. Then she had gone straight to her room to unpack the holdall which she would not, after all, be taking away with her tonight. Nor on any other night in the clandestine way she had planned. Vicente's withering scorn had seen to that. When she left the Villa now it would have to be after a frank facing of Benno with what she knew. She would beg him to let her go with dignity, and when she had gone it couldn't matter to her whether or not Vicente ever learned how wrong his judgment of her had been. As it did matter now, with a deep, rankling hurt . . .

Tania had gone down to the *salotto* to await Fabia's return, praying that Vicente might arrive first. Unable to settle, she had paced the room, opened books and closed them, poured herself a drink and discarded it after the first sip; trembled uncontrollably when she heard Fabia's car, but had forced herself to greet the older woman with a brief, would-be optimistic account of the accident.

Fabia's handsome face had blanched at the news, but the aristocratic reserve which Tania had never quite penetrated came to the aid of her control, and to the girl's guilty shame, she showed more concern for Tania than for herself.

No, she had dined well, she said. But Tania hadn't eaten? Then she must. But when Tania had claimed, shuddering, that she couldn't, Fabia didn't press her.

'Presently you will, when Vicente brings good news of Benno—or even brings Benno home with him,' she consoled. And after that they sat together, making desultory talk between long silences while they waited for Vicente.

Once Fabia said, 'I blame Benno for going out in the evening without you, *cara*.' And again: 'I hope this won't mean we must postpone your marriage,' wringing Tania's conscience cruelly.

And then Vicente came, crossing the room to Fabia, who ran to meet him.

'Vicente—what?' she faltered. He put an arm about her shoulders and drew her to him. But it was to Tania, who hadn't stirred, that he spoke.

'Benno is dead,' he said.

CHAPTER TWO

DURING the days which followed Tania was to experience the full sad pomp of Italian family mourning. Fabia went completely into black and sent for her own dressmaker to measure Tania for the mourning which, as dead Benno's intended bride, she must wear at his funeral. All the many branches of the Massimo line as far afield as France, Switzerland and Sardinia had to be notified, so that each might send at least one mourner to represent them, and there was a continual stream of local callers leaving condolence cards and flowers at the Villa.

For Tania the climate of falsehood in which Vicente had forced her to live was almost unbearable. After that first bewildering evening, she had not expected he would demand that she continue the masquerade he had forced upon her to save Fabia the double shock of Benno's accident and of her decision to break with him. She had thought that within hours, and certainly the next day, he would have told Fabia the truth and she would have been allowed to slip away quietly before the gathering of their relatives and the pageant of the funeral made the falsity of the situation intolerable for all three of them.

But as was shown by Fabia's unchanged

manner with Tania, he had said nothing to disillusion her, and when Tania confronted him to demand that she be allowed to leave before the funeral, he was adamant in his refusal.

'As far as Madrigna and the family and the mourners are to know, Benno was a happily engaged man when he died, and there is to be no whispered scandal put about that there was anything wrong between you; that you jilted him without a hearing and took yourself off as soon as his death gave you your freedom without question,' he ruled.

'But when I go, you'll have to tell your stepmother the truth, or let me tell her. And after I've gone how can it matter what scandal people talk about me?' she urged.

'My dear girl,' his short laugh was unpleasant, 'disabuse yourself, do, of the idea that I am concerned about any embarrassment for *you*! It's Benno's honour I care about. *I* may know the blame for the circumstances of his death is yours, but as I can hardly shout that from the housetops, once let the word of a rift get round, there'll be plenty of busybodies claiming "There's no smoke without fire", and that the fault was Benno's. And that I will *not* have.'

Goaded, Tania scorned, 'I believe you'd willingly shout my guilt from the housetops—if you dared. But supposing I could tell you that Benno broke faith with me before I broke with him, what then?'

'And do you claim you could do that?'

She knew that she could, but in these first hours after his death she could not bring herself to revile Benno to his brother. The age-old code which forgave the dead the mischief they had done must keep her silent, and though with a word she could blunt both Vicente's and Fabia's fond memories of Benno, she must not utter it.

With Vicente she fenced, 'If I could, would you believe me?'

'Almost certainly not, or you would have voiced your real or imagined grievance before this. You'd have given Benno a chance to defend himself. Instead you dismissed him—"I'm afraid I don't love you. Sorry you've been troubled"—and ran away. Even if your letter to him had survived the crash, can you claim it was any less brutal than that?'

She said quietly, 'I hope it wasn't brutal at all. I did tell him I'd found I couldn't love him. But I told him my reasons, and that I was going away without seeing him again because I thought it was best.'

'You thought it was "best"!' Vicente mocked her. 'And by the hindsight of what happened that same night, do you still think it was "best"?'

'I couldn't know he was going to be killed!'

'Correction—you couldn't know he was going to court death for despair of you, don't you mean?' Vicente seemed to bite deep on every word.

'He didn't——!'

'Didn't love you enough to be driven to it?'

'He didn't mean to kill himself. You dare not suggest he did!'

'Possibly not. One can't know—now. But though my own passionate reaction would have been, rather, an urge to kill *you*, I still hold you responsible for the recklessness of a mood which couldn't care whether or not it happened.' Vicente watched as horrified tears sprang to Tania's eyes and rolled down her cheeks. He said, 'So you can cry? I'd wondered. I'm afraid you will find tears expected of you tomorrow at the funeral. Which you will attend—*please*—on my orders.'

For the funeral the house was full and the last of the family mourners did not leave until two or three days later. At the funeral and while she was busy with them, Fabia bore up well, but as the villa emptied again she claimed Tania's support in a way which tore at the girl's conscience.

'I am a lonely woman,' she confided sadly. 'Vicente—he is Crystos, and that is all. He is a man—oh yes, with a man's needs, you understand. But he has never allowed an affair to dominate him nor to intrude, and he would never expect me to meet any woman he did not mean to marry. And Benno—though for Benno Crystos only meant money of which, poor boy, he never had enough—was a wild one, always out and at parties with his boy and girl-friends until he met you, *cara*, and was enchanted. But what would you?—he was young, as I think Vicente never was, and I could not expect him to stay often at home for the little free time which Vicente allowed him. I was too old to have children when I married their father, so that when Benno brought you to us, so rapturously in love with you, I was able to count on your company and the children you and Benno would have—only for there to be nothing of that for me or for you. Except that you will marry another man, though I shall still be—alone.'

Her tears would flow and Tania did her best to comfort her.

'Vicente will marry, and in time you will have his children to love,' she said.

'But that may not be until he thinks it his duty to have sons to follow him at Crystos, and I may not like any woman he chooses for duty's sake,' said Fabia with simple logic, adding, 'Besides, I am not so old now that you and I could not be like sisters, which now we shall never be. But you will stay with us for a while? Vicente thinks you should.'

If he did, it was for his own purposes, thought Tania. For the same reason that he had insisted she play her false part at Benno's funeral, he would see that she kept up the fiction for as long after it as her role of Benno's bereaved fiancée carried conviction to his friends. The scandal of her jilting Benno and her attempted escape must not rear its ugly head.

There was, for instance, the incident of her engagement ring which she had not worn since the night of Benno's death, and which she meant to give to Fabia when she left the Villa. She did not think either Fabia or Vicente had noticed its

absence from her finger until one day Fabia questioned, 'Why do you not still wear Benno's ring?
Vicente thinks you should.'

Vicente thought she should, when he knew very
well she had broken her engagement before Benno
died! How dared he? But because compassion forbade her to tell Fabia the truth in these early days
of her shock, she said, 'I didn't think I ought,
now that I'm not engaged any more, and I
thought you might like to have it.'

But Fabia shook her head. 'No, no. Even if you
feel you cannot bear to wear it again yet, you must
keep it in remembrance of Benno. But I think it
would please Vicente if you would wear it now,
while we are still in mourning for him.'

The ring went back on to Tania's hand that
day, and if Vicente noticed that it was not on her
engagement finger, he made no comment.

Meanwhile, far from forgetting the last words
she had heard Benno utter, she seemed to etch
them more deeply into her memory every day,
wincing inwardly at the cruelty from which she
had fled headlong into Vicente's clutches, and
questioning their significance as bewilderedly as
ever.

Who was the 'Pascale' to whom Benno had been
so cynically frank about his motives for courting
her? Did either Fabia or Vicente know him for a
friend of Benno's? And Sophia Greniere? Did
they know *her*? Had either Pascale or Sophia been
at Benno's funeral, both of them strangers to herself, but both of them learning, if they did not

know before, who *she* was in relation to Benno?
Knowing what they did, had either of them dared
to laugh at her? Even if not, she could hardly hope
for their pity.

And there was the enigma of Benno's claim that
he had only wooed her for some hope of gain of
which she had no inkling. He had sounded so
confident, but he must have been wrong in that!
True, she had been only too willing for him to go
through her father's business papers and settle his
affairs. But there could have been nothing in the
remains of that failed enterprise which could have
raised such hopes. There would have been debts
to be settled and a few assets realised. For the
rest, only a welter of drafts on Reggio Morre's
half-conceived and abandoned schemes and ideas,
Tania knew. Just so much waste paper which, for
sentiment's sake, she had asked Benno to pack and
bring with them when they came over to Italy
together. He had taken charge of them and they
must be among his effects still. She must ask
Vicente to return them to her when she decided
his demands of her for propriety's sake had been
served well enough. And that time could not be
far ahead . . .

She had been doing some errands for Fabia in
the city one morning when, with time to spare
before returning to the Piazzale Roma where
Rietti, the Massimo chauffeur, had left the car,
she ordered coffee on the Square of San Marco,
and watched the ever-shifting kaleidoscope of the
passers-by, the sightseers, the pedlars, the chil-

dren, the young lovers entwined, the youths strolling alone too slowly for any other purpose, she guessed, than to measure their chances of a pretty pick-up. She realised that she herself, alone at her table, was the object of some speculative glances, but she was not prepared for the long open stare of a young, blond-bearded man at a nearby table.

She looked away, then looked back; he was still intent upon her. She picked up her bag, annoyed at being forced to leave before she had meant to, but before she could move he had left his table and come over to her.

He answered in Italian the silent question of her raised eyebrows. 'Excuse me, *signorina*, but did I not see you at the funeral of my friend Benno Massimo?' And then, more slowly in English, 'You understand me? If not, I do speak your language a little, as you see. May I introduce myself, Pascale Fedore? And join you for a few minutes?'

'Pascale'—delivered into her hands! Tania said, 'You seem to know who I am, and that I'm English. But I speak Italian and I understood you very well, *signore*.'

'Then I may speak in it?'

'For whatever you need to say to me,' she replied discouragingly.

'Ah——' He sat down and gestured at her coffee-cup. 'I may order you another *cappuccino*?'

'No, thank you. I was just leaving.'

'But you will stay while I explain myself? You

see, I knew you were English, because at Benno's funeral you were pointed out to me as having been engaged to him. And your name I already knew— Tania Morre—a half-English girl with an Italian name, Benno had told me. It was your father who was Italian, I think? But he and your mother are dead?'

(That's right. You know me for a straw-coloured orphan, a nonentity to be married for a mythical fortune, thought Tania.) Aloud she said, 'I've been in Italy for the last three months or so, and if you were really a friend of Benno's, I don't understand why I never met you in that time.'

'Because I've been abroad for nearly a year, representing my firm in North America. Like Massimo, we are also in the glass trade, Vetro Mestiere, and Benno and I met at our trade college.'

'And who pointed me out to you at the funeral?'

'Someone. I——' He checked.

'You must know who it was?'

'Yes. A—woman friend of Benno's, Signora Sophia Greniere.'

'A married woman?' (And Benno's mistress!)

'Separated from her husband.'

'Whom I don't remember having met either.'

'No. Except for Benno, I don't think she was known to his family. But she had seen you with Benno at a distance, I think.'

'I see. And what was in your mind when you recognised me and decided to speak to me, *sig-*

nore? What do you want of me?'

He looked at her through frank, surprisingly light eyes. 'Nothing *of* you, *signorina*,' he said. 'Simply to offer you my sympathies over Benno, and to—get to know you a little better.'

'Better than what?' she demanded unhelpfully.

He smiled in wry apology. 'Of course you had to ask that! I meant better than I knew you through Benno. He wasn't much good at describing people, and I'm afraid he didn't do you justice in what he said of you to me. For I find you—rather lovely. Sad for Benno, but lovely. Do you mind my saying this to you, *signorina*?'

'Perhaps I shouldn't mind, if I thought you had any cause for meaning it. As it is——'

The fact that he could blush warmed her slightly to him. She added, 'But thank you, all the same. And I'm glad you spoke to me.'

Somehow she was, if only because he wasn't a Massimo for whom she had to live a lie. He knew Benno for the cheat he had been, and if they ever met again, she could think of that as an unspoken bond between them. But she also liked him for himself and didn't want to believe any longer her picture of him in gleeful enjoyment of Benno's confidences over the telephone. She *liked* him.

She fingered her bag again, and he came to draw out her chair.

'Must you go?' he asked.

'I have to catch the *vaporetto* at the Danieli stage.' She looked at her watch. 'It's about due.'

'I may see you on to it?' They walked together

across the square and on to the quay in front of the world-famous Danieli Hotel, where the water-bus had not yet chugged in to the landing stage. 'It won't be long, but please don't wait,' said Tania.

'Please let me.' Her companion hesitated, biting his lip. 'I wonder—if you are staying on at the Villa Massimo, shall I see you again?'

'I don't know. Do you come there?' she asked.

'I have been. Before I went abroad, to see Benno occasionally. But I really meant could I see you again alone, take you out to luncheon or dinner, perhaps?'

That was difficult to answer. She didn't want to snub him too bluntly, but she didn't know how Vicente or Fabia would react to her accepting the invitation. Nothing social at all had been planned at the Villa since Benno's death. 'I'm afraid we're still in mourning for Benno,' she reminded Pascale. 'I don't think——'

'I'm sorry. But I could at least telephone and invite you a little later——?' She wasn't attending. Her glance had gone behind him to see Vicente parting from two men at the doors of the Danieli. Evidently he had seen her too, for he crossed the quay in a purposeful stride to join her, looking a question at Pascale, who said quickly, 'Signor Massimo? Signorina Morre and I met on Piazza San Marco, and she is waiting for the *vaporetto*, which is late.'

Vicente nodded cool recognition of him. 'Yes, Fedore—Pascale Fedore, isn't it? Of Vetro

Mestiere? I haven't seen you for a long time.'

'No, I've been abroad. I knew Benno well. I'm—sorry, *signore*.'

'Ah, thank you.' Vicente turned to Tania. 'No need for you to wait for the *vaporetto*. I have the launch here. You are on your way home, I gather?' Without a further word to Pascale, he took her by the elbow and led her down the steps to the launch basin. She looked back with a shrug of apology for Pascale, who mouthed, 'I will call you one day,' and watched them go.

Vicente took the wheel of his private launch, steering it skilfully among the lunchtime craft on the Canal. When they were under way in mid-stream, Tania said, 'That was a bit abrupt of you, wasn't it? You know him, and he knew me. He didn't pick me up.'

'How was it that he knew you? Had Benno introduced him to you?'

'No. He was at Benno's funeral, and I was pointed out to him.'

'And on the Piazza?'

'I was having coffee at a table, and he came over.'

'What for?'

'To introduce himself as a friend of Benno's, and to offer us his sympathy.'

'Which he should have done by calling to leave his card upon Madrigna, like our other friends, instead of making questionable advances to you,' Vicente ruled sententiously.

Tania stared at the granite profile turned to her.

'Questionable advances'?' she echoed. 'He only came and spoke to me, for pity's sake!'

'And stayed to chat, and escorted you to the quay. And issued some ongoing invitations to this or that?'

'He did ask me to dine with him some time, yes,' she returned defiantly.

'And you said——?'

'That we are still in mourning for Benno, because I didn't know whether his mother or you would care for me to accept.'

At the end of the launch's run Vicente stood up, helped her out and moored the launch before he answered that. Then he said, 'You were right to suppose we shouldn't care for it, and neither should you. And though your mourning for Benno isn't as sincere or deep-felt as ours, if you do feel free to encourage the young man in future, may I hope you won't flaunt him as your conquest in front of our friends?'

He went ahead of her to where she had told him Rietti would be waiting with the car, put her into it and left them to pick up his own car.

All the way back to the Villa Tania was fuming inwardly. Even if Vicente still held her responsible for Benno's death, what right had he to dictate her conduct like that? His attitude was positively feudal, and it bore out all she had heard about the honour and standing of the family being the Italian all-in-all. She mustn't smirch it by being seen with another man so soon after Benno's death. That had been Vicente's edict to her when, far from being a member of his family, she wasn't even his sister-in-law! Well, she wanted and needed to see Pascale Fedore again, if only to find out whether his friendly interest in her was genuine or mere curiosity about the girl he knew had been Benno's dupe. Besides, he knew Sophia Greniere, and there should be a bitter kind of satisfaction in probing Pascale about her too.

And so, Vicente Massimo, Tania addressed him mentally, I'm afraid you're going to have to lock me up, if I'm not to see whom I please! Though even as she framed her defiance of him, she suspected that, given provocation, he would be capable even of that.

Meanwhile she had to tackle him on the return of those papers of her father's which he must have taken over when clearing up Benno's affairs. Expecting him to make no difficulty about handing them over, she asked him for them casually one day, only to be met by his blank denial that he had them.

'You mean your father's death certificate? His will?' he asked.

'No. I have those.'

'What else, then?'

'The business papers he left behind when he died. Unfinished business, mostly, schemes which never went through. Benno sorted them and went over them and said they were of no value to anyone but me. But I wanted to keep them, and they came over with us from England, I know,' she said.

Vicente shook his head. 'I found no papers relating to your father's affairs among Benno's things,' he said.

'But he *had* them. He only took charge of them for me. He knew I should want them back!' Tania protested in puzzled distress.

'He must have misunderstood you and destroyed them. They were valueless, you say?'

'Yes. Just jotted ideas for sales promotions, things like that; schemes he never carried out. Benno's check confirmed that for mė. But all the same——' She broke off, scorning to look to Vicente to understand mere sentiment, but at least expecting his apology on Benno's behalf, which did not come.

He said, 'I'll make another search, but I do assure you I missed nothing of that sort the first time. Are you quite sure Benno didn't give them back to you himself?'

She did manage to look her scorn of that suggestion, and with a murmured, 'Thank you. If you would——' she left him, but not escaping the dark suspicion forming in her mind. Supposing——?

Supposing, against all her own belief and his assurances, Benno *had* found something of potential value among Reggio's papers—the 'goldmine' of which he was convinced she was ignorant, but of which he had been confident enough to boast about it to Pascale?

She couldn't guess what it was, nor what could be of even passing interest to a world-famous competitor like Crystos of Venice, and thinking back to that fatal telephone talk with Pascale, she remembered that Benno had said Vicente had shown only a lacklustre interest in the scheme Benno had lauded.

But supposing her father *had* lighted upon, without pursuing, some revolutionary development in the glass industry? Supposing Vicente, sorting through Benno's effects, had discovered the relevant papers and had changed his mind to be fired with the same enthusiasm as Benno for the possibilities of the idea—what might have been his reaction?

If he were honest, surely to share with her what he had learned.

If he were not, and believed he had reason to hate and despise her, mightn't he have done just what her suspicion of him told he had done— destroyed the evidence out of hand and denied to her that it had ever existed?

At the thought she went physically cold, beads of sweat came out on her brow and her top lip, and her throat worked, as if she had to fight vomit. If Vicente Massimo had done this to her, she would——! But though she struggled to express an ultimate of revenge against him, nothing in her power seemed adequate. She *had* no power to wield against him. Only suspicion without proof which would take her nowhere; only her word against his, and if accusing questions were ever asked, he could always claim, rightly, that she had admitted the papers had no value. But as she writhed with frustration she made one resolve. Until then she had been counting the days until Italian ideas of seemliness in a bereaved fiancée would let her leave the Villa. She supposed that Vicente would indicate when she could consider herself free to go. But now she was going to be in no special hurry. Now she would be willing to wait a little while she watched and listened and sought a chink in her enemy's armour. Never in her life had a man so roused her. She had been hurt and then contemptuous of Benno's perfidy, but they had been weak reactions compared with this dawning and then growing fascination—yes, fascination!—of waging conflict against Vicente Massimo, of thwarting his will for her at least with the opposing dumb insolence of her own, even if she could do no more.

Her first opportunity came with the sound of the telephone. There were bedside extensions to every room, and when no one else answered it, she picked up her receiver. . . .

After the austerity of respecting Fabia's ideas of suitable mourning clothes, it had been pleasant to dress for going out to dinner with Pascale Fedore. In her mood of defiance Tania had been tempted to choose scarlet, but for Fabia's sake had compromised with ballet-length filmy green and a silver-grey stole for her shoulders. After her meeting with Pascale she had told Fabia about him; Fabia remembered him vaguely as a friend of Benno's, and when he had called for her this evening in his car, Tania had joined him with Fabia's blessing, she thought. Vicente had not been at home.

They had driven to Padua by the river road to dine in a Palladian villa converted to a restaurant in the old part of the city. Inevitably, with Benno as their common link, they had talked about him, and at one point she had been tempted to tell Pascale the truth about her break with Benno and its reason. He had suggested that she must miss Benno a lot, and perhaps her 'Yes, of course', had sounded too lukewarm, for he had pressed her, 'You did love him, didn't you?' which she had fended off with her own question, 'Why do you ask?'

Pascale had said earnestly, 'I suppose, because I rather wanted to know that you weren't simply bewitched by his charm. He was rather practised in it, I'm afraid, and it had a devastating effect which I should hate to think he had used on you.'

Was he warning her of something he couldn't guess she already knew about Benno? She fenced carefully, 'But doesn't one always want and ask to be bewitched when one is in love? Or, being a man, wouldn't you know?'

'Oh, I'd know,' he assured her quickly. With a look which hinted he was enjoying it now, he added, 'It's a delightful experience. But it isn't all of love, is it, as I think Benno had found when he didn't marry any of the girls he had known before you.'

'Was there one in particular before me?'

Pascale sidestepped that adroitly. 'You forget, I was abroad until just before the accident. After I came back, the first time we were in touch was by telephone on the actual day he was killed.'

'Did he tell you anything about me then?'

'Yes. He described you, said he had brought you over from England to be married from the Villa, as your parents were dead.'

Poor Pascale! Doing his best to sound loyal to Benno, not knowing she knew he was gilding the truth, thought Tania. Taking pity on him, she changed the subject, surprised to find that her resentment of Benno's betrayal of her was less bitter than her venom against Vicente's measured spite. Benno hadn't lived to carry out his mischief against her. From the very hour of Benno's death, Vicente had begun to work on his.

Pascale opened his car for the drive back in the gentle night air. At the Villa she asked him to go in with her, but he refused, saying he wouldn't intrude on Fabia. At parting he said, 'May we do this again? and kissed her lightly, and she went in, flushed and windblown, to find Vicente alone in the *salotto*. This she had expected—Fabia usually went to bed early—and she could have gone herself straight up to her room. But Vicente's comments on what he would see as her truancy she was reluctant to miss.

But to her surprise he didn't open with overt criticism of her. He was reading papers and making notes on them and drinking wine, in

which he invited her to join him. Distrusting him
mellow as much as she distrusted him withdrawn,
she felt she should be fortified for the strictures
to come, and accepted.

As she watched him cross the room to the
drinks table she surprised herself again. He had
changed for the evening into a corded jacket and
tapering raw silk slacks, and she was forced to
allow that he was extremely handsome in a dark,
saturnine way. As he lifted the decanter and glass
and poured, he was in profile to her, and she
found her eyes drawn from the high brow to the
proud nose and the full lips, wondering if they
ever kissed in gentle homage, or whether they
lusted and took in assertive demand——

Heavens! She brought her thoughts up sharp.
Speculating on Vicente with sexual overtones?
She must be out of her mind. The man was sheer
bedrock, and for all Fabia's oblique hints as to his
male experience, Tania could not picture him
with a woman in his arms.

He brought her wine to her and watched her
over the rim of his own glass as she drank. 'You
enjoyed your evening?' he asked uncritically.

'Thank you. Very much.'

'Feeling you could afford to flout my advice to
keep a low profile, and asserting your right to
choose your own occasions?'

Here it came—this *was* criticism! She said, 'I
simply accepted Pascale Fedore's invitation to
dine with him. I didn't even consider debating
with you whether I should or not.'

'He brought you home, but you didn't ask him in?'

'I did ask him, but he refused.'

'You shouldn't have allowed him to refuse. Dropping you on the doorstep is conduct only meted out to housemaids in our society.'

Tania compressed her lips. 'I'm sorry. I didn't realise your rules of etiquette were quite so rigid— or so outdated. In England, where housemaids exist at all, they are treated like anyone else. And Pascale refused to come in with me out of consideration for your stepmother.'

'Pascale?' Vicente's brows went up. 'On first name terms already?'

'That's present-day usage too, didn't you know?'

He ignored that and went to stand facing her, glass in one hand, the other arm bent to support him on the mantelshelf. 'You know, don't you, that your escort is a member of our chief trade competitors?'

'Vetro Mestiere? Yes, what of it?'

He shrugged. 'Nothing particularly. Only that impudent assumptions could be made of your association with Fedore.'

'Assumptions—such as?'

'For instance, that one of us, either Crystos or Vetro Mestiere, might be angling for a merger or a takeover. Than which nothing need be further from the truth, but which could be disastrous for our shares while the stock market debated it.'

Tania stared and laughed—a mistake, as she

read from his darkened expression. 'Just because Pascale Fedore has taken me out to dinner, you have to be afraid of the business consequences? Oh, really——!' she mocked him. 'I'm almost flattered!'

For answer he strode over to her, took her half-finished drink from her and set down the glass out of her reach. 'Now you're being silly,' he said. 'Martini-silly or whisky-silly, I shouldn't wonder——'

'How dare you imply——?' She was near enough to him to slap his face, but he had pinioned both her wrists.

'—that your escort plied you with too much liquor while he had you?' he finished for her. 'Because your hysteria makes it rather apparent, is why I dare, and why I'm not giving you any more. I instance—reasonably enough, if you knew our greedy gossip columnists as I do—the possible consequences of a continued association with Fedore. You, ripe for a quarrel, accuse me of making too much of an isolated incident, whereas I am merely asking that you—what is the current jargon?—cool it a little, lest the situation get out of hand.'

But Vicente 'asking' was Vicente threatening, she knew. 'And supposing I don't cool it?' she demanded. 'Supposing I choose to see Pascale Fedore again whenever he asks me?'

If she expected an overt threat, it did not come. 'Ah, but I think you won't,' he said confidently. 'In your right mind, you will see the reason and common courtesy of meeting me in this.'

'Don't you mean when I'm sober?' she flashed.

'Possibly.' He let the single word convey its insult. Then he went to the door and switched off the room lights one by one. His finger on the last, 'Meanwhile, if you aren't to be compromised by remaining with me in the dark, if I were you I should go to bed,' he advised, his tone deceptively mild.

She went. See Pascale again after *that*? Of course she would! And did—three more times without any comment from Vicente, until on the third occasion Pascale told her their next meeting must be their last for a time as he was being sent abroad again on another publicity trip for his firm.

'South America, this time. Moving around, "no settled address". But you will keep in touch, won't you?' he begged.

'Whenever you can tell me where to reach you,' she promised. 'How long will you be away?'

'Not as long as last time. Three months at the outside.'

'By which time I probably shan't be here.' (How long *might* it take to trap Vicente, if she could?)

'Oh!' Pascale was startled. 'Where, then?'

'In England again, I expect. You know I only stayed on to help Signora Massimo over a difficult time,' she reminded him.

'And yourself too, I suppose,' he suggested compassionately, adding as he reached for her hand across their luncheon table, 'You mustn't resent this, but you can't know how often I've wished that *I* had met you before Benno did!'

And you can't know how bitterly I have to wish that I'd never met Benno at all, Tania thought as she pressed Pascale's fingers in grateful return.

He was to telephone her the time and place of their last date on the evening when he was to catch a late night train for Genoa and his flight. When she had heard nothing from him that same day, she was puzzled but concluded he had been too busy to ring. By five o'clock she was genuinely worried. The maids said there had been no message for her, though one of them said she had been taking a call earlier from, she believed, Signor Fedore, when '*il signore*', as the staff called Vicente, had taken the receiver from her and dismissed her.

Tania was furious. It was Sunday, Vicente had been at home all day and could easily have put Pascale through to her or passed on his message. That he had done neither meant that he was deliberately interfering, and that she would *not* have. As she went in search of him she wondered that Pascale had not rung again. Or perhaps he had, and Vicente had managed to intercept that call too.

Vicente had a study which he used when he worked at home. He was there; its door was open and he seemed to have expected her when she knocked and went in.

'I understand Pascale Fedore telephoned today

with a message for me which he would have given to you,' she said. If Mitzi, the maid, weren't mistaken, he would have to admit it!

But standing to face her, he said levelly, 'Fedore did ring and I did answer him, but he wished to leave no message for you.'

'But—but we had a provisional date! For tonight. He's going abroad at dawn. He was to ring me to confirm times——!' In her bewilderment at Vicente's cool denial she felt the distant dignity with which she had meant to deal with him slipping away from her.

He was saying, 'Yes, so he told me. But after I had told him something he didn't know and at which he was considerably upset, he said he did not want to see you again, nor to have any written or spoken contact with you in the future.'

'But what could you have told him, for him to reject me like that? Not—not that you knew I'd broken with Benno before he died? You haven't wanted that known!' she protested.

Vicente shook his head. 'No, not that. I told him that, since Benno's death, you and I had reached an understanding, and that you are unofficially engaged to me.'

CHAPTER THREE

TANIA stared in horrified disbelief. Almost choking on the words, she stammered, 'You—you can't have told Pascale a lie like that, just to keep him from seeing me again! It would have been—*monstrous*. Anyway, he wouldn't have believed you!'

'You think not? Though if I didn't convince him, why should he have decided for himself that he wanted nothing more to do with you?' Vicente questioned, as if reason were on his side, not hers.

'He couldn't—wouldn't have told you that!'

'I assure you he did. Not surprisingly, surely, once he suspected you have been keeping dark your commitment to me, while carrying on with him? A very transparent young man, Fedore. I could see him wondering when you had meant to come clean with him, or whether you hoped to keep him dangling on a string after we were married.'

Tania gasped. 'You could see nothing of the sort! We liked each other, but we were only friends——'

'Good friends?'

'—and I've only to get in touch with him to contradict anything you may have told him.'

'And how do you propose to reach him?'

'Before he catches the train for Genoa.'

'Unfortunately he decided, in the circumstances, to leave by an earlier train. He has gone by now.'

'I'll have him paged at the airport.'

Vicente nodded. 'Do that—and swallow your pride when he refuses to answer to the paging, which in his present mood, I think he will. However, no doubt you have addresses that will find him on his travels?'

Though Tania knew her silence was an admission that she had to wait for Pascale to get in touch with her, she said nothing, and Vicente went on, 'And of course he will be coming back to Venice with the spoils of his salesmanship, and, if not earlier, you will be able to plead your case with him then.' He paused before adding, 'Always supposing that by that time you will have any valid case for proving me a liar. You see what I mean?'

'I don't, I'm afraid. You did lie—outrageously!'

'I'd prefer to call it anticipating fact.'

'Fact? What fact?' Tania dared not let herself understand.

'The present fact of our doing it, I hope. As I've said—no lie; simply a manipulation of a truth which should be undeniable by the time Fedore returns.'

Now she couldn't escape his meaning. 'You must be—be insane to suggest such a thing,' she burst out. 'You—marry me? I marry you? Why, you've distrusted me and ranged yourself against me ever since Benno died! And what do you suppose that's done for me against you? Made me hate you—*hate* you, do you hear?'

Imperturbably he said, 'That's a pity. Perhaps inevitable in a near-hysteric like you. But not incurable, since by the very nature of a normal marriage—and I'm sure you know what I mean?—it's impossible to be at loggerheads all the time. Every night, that is, as well as all day.'

Tania felt that the deep flush which burned in her face was a tangible thing, enveloping her whole body. 'A marriage between you and me wouldn't be a marriage at all,' she muttered.

'Ah, but it has to be. If not in the relationship you and Benno achieved and which you chose to reject, at least in the essentials which the very word means. Nature isn't very concerned with the loving kindness in a marriage, you know—only with the continuation of the species. But you find that crude?' Vicente insinuated.

He must know she did, and she couldn't tell why she stayed to listen or to argue with him. But something impelled her to try to understand the twisted purpose behind his bizarre proposal. She began, 'You suggest marriage to me within weeks of Benno's death, and I suppose I have to believe you're serious——'

'I am.'

'Then what becomes of your argument that I mustn't be seen in the company of another man so soon, let alone become engaged to him? If I let you persuade me to it, what kind of scandal could your circle of friends make of *that*?'

'The man in the case being myself—Benno's brother—they could make no scandal.'

'You're doubling back on what you told me to keep me here for a "decent" time!' she accused. 'And what about your stepmother? How would she view a marriage—in cold blood—to me?'

Vicente said, 'She has viewed it. And she approves.'

'You've already *told* her that you——?'

'Yes, listen——'

'You had no right! I *won't* listen!'

'You will.' Swiftly he moved to the open door, shut it and stood with his back to it. 'Now—' his dark eyes narrowed upon her—'you chose to ally yourself to an Italian family, and are about to hear the facts of Italian family life. In short, we value it above everything—particularly above senti-mental attachments which, as you have de-monstrated by your break with Benno, may not last. Its continuance is all-important, and if one of the threads which can ensure that is broken— as happened when Benno died—then no one is going to read scandal into the knitting in of an-other thread *from the same family*. As soon as is convenient and agreeable to both parties, though without, naturally, any overdue regard for romance.' He paused. 'You understand me, I hope?'

Though unwilling to concede any inch to him, though finding such an attitude utterly alien, Tania had to recognise the inbred faith in his family's rights and duties which went to the making of the man. In other things he might be as heartless and as devious as she half suspected he was; as Benno had *been*. But she had to respect his loyalty to this code, hidebound as it was, and so she signified that she understood him with a bow of her head.

He said tautly, 'Good. As for Madrigna, her own first marriage was arranged for her, and she came to her second, with my father, with little chance of children of her own. When Benno was engaged she hoped to enjoy at least step-grand-children, and with our marriage she can still hope. Dare you refuse her that?'

Tania claimed wildly, 'Of course I can! I must. It's *my life* you're manipulating; using me as a pawn in your own plans, when you could choose any other woman to marry you. You don't have to try to pressurise *me!*'

'You dislike the prospect so much?'

'What do you think!'

'Then I shall have to pressurise your con-science, by pointing out that it is you—not "any other woman"—who owes a heavy debt to my family.' As she flinched, he went on, 'I see I haven't to remind you of your moral re-sponsibility, with the letter you sent him which drove Benno recklessly to his death?'

'I don't accept that I owe any debt to your family over that,' she denied.

'Accept it or not, I hold you to it,' he said.

'*You* hold me to it! Who are you, Vicente Massimo, that you dare?' she demanded.

Unmoved by her vehemence, his lips barely parting to frame the words, 'I am Benno's brother, with my own responsibility to his memory which I intend to carry out,' he said.

At that, at the implacable will which saw no reason but its own, Tania recognised the futility of arguing further in her defence. She asked, 'And when I say No to a proposal you could hardly hope I'd accept, I suppose you'll want me to leave as soon as possible?'

'If I thought your refusal was final, naturally. Though Madrigna is fond of you and would regret your going, your relationship with her and with myself could hardly be the same, could it?' As he spoke he moved from the door, as if he were making way for her departure from the Villa there and then. And strangely it was that gesture as of dismissal, of his having done with her, that in a flash Tania was reminded that if she left within a day or days it would be too soon for her to have had her way with him; achieved her purpose of finding him out as no less a cheat than Benno had been. Perhaps he wasn't. But she would be gone with no chance or satisfaction of knowing either way. Whereas his offer would enable her to stay, and in the daily traffic of a marriage, however bloodless, there should be opportunity to learn and deduce and put together ... If she said Yes to him, that chance of revenge would be hers.

Later she was to realise with shocked horror that she had given her resolve scarcely any thought before she heard herself telling him, 'And if my refusal weren't final, if I agreed to marry you for *your* reasons, you would have to accept that I should only say Yes to you for reasons of my own. Private ones, which you wouldn't share.'

What had she said? What had she done? She could have been out of this house and free by tomorrow at the latest, yet she had given herself into his hands for the sake of a revenge she might never achieve. She watched for his reaction, dreading his mockery of an about-turn which must have surprised him.

But if the outcome had been no more than he expected, Vicente said evenly, 'As long as you accept my terms, I'm not interested in your reasons for doing so. It's enough that you have the sense to recognise that justice demands it of you. And so, our decisions agreed, there's no point in delaying the necessary arrangements. You will hold yourself in readiness for when they are made?'

Tania longed to point out that they could not have agreed decisions if she had withheld hers. But he had taken her conditional surrender for consent, and it was too late now.

'Do you plan to marry in church?' she asked.

'Of course. But quietly, with few or no guests, which, in the circumstances, people will understand, and there will be no wedding journey, to which I can give no time.' He crossed the room to consult a diary on his desk. 'Yes, the twenty-seventh, give or take a day or two, if Padre Duchoni can make it then.' He looked up. 'That will suit you?'

'It has to, doesn't it?'

'And will you tell Madrigna our news, or shall I?'

'I will.'

As she turned to the door he went to open it for her. 'And I may trust you?'

'Trust me?'

'Not to scuttle away by night, leaving a "So sorry" note on my bureau? Such an anti-climax, if I had to forestall you a second time!'

'You won't have to. In this marriage I shall have no ideals to lose, so you can count on my standing by the letter of my word to you,' Tania replied with dignity.

'And also, I hope, to the letter of your duty as a wife? Of *all* your duties as a wife!' The implied threat followed her as she turned and left him.

The discreet announcement of their travesty of an engagement caused no more stir than Vicente had forecast it would. That the head of Crystos was about to take a bride was news in the city's business circles, but apparently there were no raised eyebrows of surprise over the short interval between Benno's death and the 'knitting in' of this new family thread. There were letters of congratulation for Vicente; the same people who had sent wedding presents to Benno and Tania and had had them returned to them sent again to Tania and Vicente, and it seemed to be generally accepted that Vicente's election for a private ceremony was the right one.

This matter-of-fact attitude was typified in Fabia's own. She saw the affair as a happy ending to a time of stress and sorrow for them all, but to Tania's relief she did not claim to believe that romance had blossomed suddenly between Tania and Vicente. She did not pretend that the marriage would be a phoenix of bliss rising for them; she was convinced that Tania still loved and would not easily forget Benno. But she was happy with the expedience of the marriage, and that she did not look for raptures of anticipation from either of them helped Tania through the hideously difficult days.

On one of them the question of Benno's engagement ring came up again. Tania begged Fabia to accept it, and this time Fabia did not demur. She said, 'Naturally you will be wearing Vicente's ring now. He asked me what stone I thought you would like, and I remembered we had agreed one day that emeralds were the loveliest. So I hope that is what he will give you.'

He did—by a method fully in keeping with their coldblooded pact, but by which Tania felt perversely cheated. She should have appreciated his tact in having the ring-case put on her dressing-table with a terse note—'If this suits you, please thank me by wearing it.' But an engagement ring should be given in tenderness and promise. She had been able to believe that even Benno's had been given so, and without the shared loving she thought they had enjoyed then, it would have been a dead thing.

As was the magnificence of this mitre-cornered

square emerald, tried on in the privacy of her own room—the symbol of a promise as coldly conceived on Vicente's side as on her own.

And now the promises had been exchanged, and the emerald was guarding the plain gold band which Vicente had put on her finger at the brief wedding ceremony, witnessed by Fabia and Padre Duchoni's curate, which was followed by a wedding breakfast, where the only guests were Fabia, the padre and the curate. The afternoon hours had been much like those of any other day, and Tania saw a desert of such empty days before her. If Benno had kept faith with her, when they married they would have taken their own house or apartment. But there had been no suggestion that Fabia would bow out from the Villa, nor that Tania should take over the reins of its management, and Tania was left to wonder how Vicente envisaged she would spend her time if, that was, he had given it any thought at all. She had had work and interests of her own ever since she had left school, and had looked forward to a life with Benno which might have room for them. But what was she to share with Vicente, for whom she would be virtually invisible, except in the role he had allotted to her, that of the biddable, submissive wife to a man of his arrogance and self-claimed power? She remembered that she had once wondered what marriage to him would be like. Now, she supposed, she was doomed to learn . . .

Last night she had slept in her own room. Today Fabia must have given orders for her per-

sonal things to be transferred to the master bedroom while they were at the church and the
wedding breakfast. For when they had returned
the exchange had been made, and Tania was now
the owner of a twin dressing-room to Vicente's,
separated from hers by their bathroom, and the
scrolled 'M' above the immense bed stood for the
'Massimo' that was hers, as she had once indulged
happy dreams that it would be.

Fabia, having tactfully arranged to dine out
herself, had arranged the dinner which Tania and
Vicente would share, tête-à-tête, and before she
went out had done her embarrassed best to advise
Tania on the evening's outcome.

They had taken their aperitifs with Vicente, and
when he had left them to go to change, she told
Tania, 'It is not always easy, the first meal together, the first—night. I, like you, *cara*, had a
young love whom I did not marry. My parents
had other plans for me, and I had to obey. And
though I know you must respect and value
Vicente, you may not be able to love him until
Benno is farther back in your past, and so the—
obligations of marriage may be as hard for you at
first as they were for me. Perhaps Vicente will
understand this, perhaps not. But he would not
have married you if he did not hope to make you
happy, and to make up to you for losing Benno as
far as he is able.'

How little of the truth about either of them
Fabia knew, Tania thought in pity and guilt. She
could only suppose that custom and experience

had taught Fabia to see nothing sinister in a marriage which had been arranged after so little courtship. She had never once questioned Tania's agreement to it, nor shown any curiosity about Pascale's dismissal from Tania's scene.

Before joining Vicente and Fabia for drinks Tania had changed for dinner into a lemon yellow dress of fine wool which she had bought for her original trousseau. She wore her hair with a centre parting and caught back at each side with a comb. For her wedding no one had suggested she should wear the white she had planned for her marriage to Benno. Instead she had worn a pale grey silk suit and a tiny hat, tiara-wise. When dressing both times she was struck by the fact that Vicente had never uttered a word of approval or otherwise of her clothes, cheating her as always of his notice, except for that basilisk, appraising stare which she could have imagined saw through to her every impulse, every thought.

He did not join her again until Fabia had left and their dinner was about to be served. They drank a dry white wine with the fish and a claret with breasts of duck in a delicious sauce, followed by an iced pudding topped with raspberries. Fabia could not cook herself, but the dishes to which she inspired her staff for special occasions were superb. For this one she had arranged for a posy of all-coloured everlasting flowers to be laid at Vicente's place, along with a bar-pin and directions to him to fasten it to the corsage of Tania's dress.

He had done so before they sat down, bending

to the task and achieving it without fumbling. For the few moments he was about it, he was more intimately close to her than he had yet been, except for his formal kiss after their marriage ceremony. And while his hands were busy and his dark head bent to the level of her breasts, she was physically stirred by his nearness, tensed and aware that even the light touch of his fingers was exciting her against her will. She wondered if he had noticed the pounding of her heart. Any other man would have done; Benno would have made playful capital out of it. But Vicente? No!

Tania had resolved that as soon as she was able, she would begin her probe into whatever had tempted him—if anything had—to conceal his knowledge of the contents of her father's papers. But their first evening of marriage seemed hardly the time, and she let him choose easy openings for their talk over dinner—of local events and people and the excellent food.

He had a knack—she had noticed it before, when his hands were at rest on a flat surface, of putting a forefinger to climb over the middle one, leaving it to rest there in the casual manner of a crossed knee. It was unique to him. Between courses he was doing it tonight on the table. He had fine hands, long-fingered, and the curious thought struck Tania that if it were possible to love a man's hands without loving the man, she would fall for Vicente's.

After dinner they watched a documentary programme on television. It dealt with peasant life in

Southern Italy, and when it was over Vicente threw several interesting sidelights on the subject. The two of them might have been friends who had dined and gone to a lecture together, Tania felt. Was it possible Vicente shared none of her own anticipatory hopes and fears of the night ahead?

At last he said he would smoke a cigar in the garden—which she took to mean he considered the evening over. Their room was softly lighted in readiness for their coming, the bed turned down, curtains drawn, towels warming in the bathroom. When Vicente came up he used a door from the corridor into his dressing-room, and when he came through to the bedroom he was already in a hip-length robe, open to its waist sash. He crossed to the bedside where Tania, who had showered and lingered over her undressing, was standing barefoot in her nightgown of gauzy lawn. She reached for its matching negligé, but he forestalled her by drawing her down to sit on the bed, beside him.

He said, not making it a question, 'You are frightened.'

She nodded Yes.

'Of me?'

Again, 'Yes.'

'Even though, between you and me, this—' from his gesture she knew what he meant—'could be regarded as a mere extra seal on this morning's ceremony, and you weren't nervous then?'

'This is—different.'

'How so? For us it's no more than another

clause in a civil contract, drawn up to suit our purpose. I'd have thought you'd have a good deal more to fear from the first night of a love marriage —lest you should disappoint your man; lest you find him a poorer lover than you hoped. But perhaps your "first night" with Benno had no strings to it? *Was* he your lover while you were engaged?'

'No!' She drew away from him, frowning.

'Nor Pascale Fedore? Nor any man before either of them——?'

'No. What right have you to ask me?' Emboldened by her indignation, she demanded, 'I could as well want to know how many women *you* have had before you married me!'

'You could indeed,' Vicente allowed. 'And if I cared what you thought of me, I should give you the answer which should please you. Conversely, if I didn't give a fig for your opinion of me, I should probably tell you the truth.'

'And which are you telling me?'

He laughed dryly. 'Neither,' he said. 'Come here.'

Tania did not stir, but he drew closer. He put an arm round her shoulders and tilted her chin with a fingertip. 'We could try to make it a pleasurable second clause,' he murmured, and kissed her closed lips slowly, tempting them to respond.

She must have known that something like this would happen, but she could not believe that it had; that Vicente the cold, controlled enigma, could so go through the motions of lovemaking without a shred of warm feeling for her behind it.

When his hands moved in restless exploration, untied the confining ribbons of her nightgown, smoothed her flesh while his lips demanded hers bruisingly, she wondered whose body his imagination was fantasising in her place.

It was difficult for her lips not to stir beneath his, and when they parted moistly, he gave a small chuckle of satisfaction, as if he had breached a wall between himself and her. He continued to kiss her seductively, then laid her back upon the bed, kneeling above her, barring any way of escape.

Her will was urging, *Push him away. Show him how unschooled, how unready you are to make love where you don't love.* But her body, pleasured by the sensuous touch of his hands tracing the line of her rib-cage, the curve of her waist, the swell of her thighs, refused to obey. And when he allowed his weight to press more closely upon its softness, her body did not want to obey her will. This was now, the intimate contact of flesh with flesh which she had never known before, but virgin and reluctant as she was, her woman's instinct was answering the call of the male, eagerly receptive of all it might ask of her. In those moments of her yielding to him, the enemy who was Vicente Massimo was no more than a shadow without threat. The invitation of her answering desire was not for him but for his body's arousing of her, and when his experienced lovemaking turned to the sudden lust of passion, she was ardent, welcoming, and oblivious of the brief, sharp stab of the pain of her complete acceptance of him.

On the sweet downward surge of aftermath her senses were clamouring that *this* body's claim upon her she would always accept, but it was with shock that she plummeted to the earth of realising whose body it was, and how little it must have meant to him to enslave her so.

At the thought she turned on her side with a little moan, humiliated tears squeezing slowly from beneath her lids. She waited. What now? If Vicente were kind, she couldn't bear it. If he were not, so much the easier to hate him again. As if he read her thoughts he moved to lean over the shoulder she had turned to him.

'What did I tell you?' he asked in a voice with no trace now of pent, excited breath. 'Hating is for daytime and we can go back to it tomorrow. Tonight we've enjoyed each other sexually, and shall again. So go to sleep now. You are over your worst hurdle.'

But of course sleep was not for her. She heard him go into his dressing-room and waited, tensed, for him to come back. But he did not come. She remembered then that there was a narrow bed in his dressing-room, and realised that he meant to leave her alone for the night.

CHAPTER FOUR

THE merciful oblivion of sleep came at last, and when she woke it was morning. For a few bemused moments it was a morning like any other. Then it became the first morning of her marriage to Vicente and a prospect to be more dreaded than any yet in her life.

Before Benno had betrayed her she had wondered what the first day of their honeymoon would be like. They would have joked and teased and pretended not to be looking forward to its being night again. They would have been the same pair of young lovers as had made love overnight. They wouldn't be the two different people which she and Vicente would be this morning. Last night Vicente had 'known' her in the Biblical sense, seducing her need to love and to express love by binding her to him with a physical tie which he had previously dismissed as a mere 'clause in a contract'.

He had acted the lover, yes. That had been part of his skill, and she had fallen, bewitched and willing victim enough. And almost—*almost*, he had convinced her of his own need of her. Hadn't he used the word 'enjoy' of their coupling and hadn't he promised it would happen again? But of course he meant it should; he had warned her of it when he had reminded her of her total duty as a wife. As for his enjoyment of her, could he have meant more by that than that he had relished his male power over her? No. And No again to the possibility that last night had changed or bettered anything between them. Today they would be the hostile strangers they were yesterday and would be tomorrow. And even if her body again said Yes to his as eagerly and treacherously as it had last night, *she* could hold herself as aloof from him as ever . . .

Vicente was to make the aloofness easy. When he came, dressed, into her room at the same time as her early coffee, he was practising some reserves of his own. He did not even ask her how she had slept, but as soon as the maid had gone, began to discuss—of all things!—his financial plans for her future.

'I am sending Signor Bertolli, my man of business, to see you this morning with the details of how my settlement on you is invested, your current allowance and so on,' he said. 'I've made his appointment for eleven, so be at home for him, will you?'

Tania had to swallow hard on her revulsion against accepting anything from him. 'In the circumstances, is a settlement necessary?' she asked.

'Of course, since it will include my provision for your children in the event of my death,' he snapped.

'An allowance, then? Yet at least, I mean. I still have funds from my father's estate for anything I need.'

'Enough to finance your position as my wife? Nonsense,' Vicente dismissed. 'Would you like to apply for a driving test and have your own car?'

Her everyday expenses she might have to accept, but she would *not* take a car from him. 'No, thank you,' she said.

'Very well. You must use Rietti to drive you into the city, and Madrigna will enjoy taking you about with her. By the way, please call her Madrigna, as she is now your stepmother too. Is there anything else you would like to have settled at the moment?'

He might have been closing a business interview with a question which he was confident would not be answered in the affirmative. Tania had the impression that he wasn't even interviewing *her*, but just anyone at all with problems to be solved. Yet last night—— But she must not think of last night. 'Yes,' she said, and saw him frown as at an impertinence. 'I'd like to know what you expect me to do from now on; how to fill my time?'

'How? Why, as you've done hitherto, I suppose,' he replied.

'While I've been your guest?'

'Why not, except that your status will be different and that from time to time you will be doing some social and business entertaining for me. And as soon as Madrigna thinks it suitable to invite them, you will be meeting our friends. But tell me,' he added cruelly, 'what was your idea of the married life you would lead with Benno before you decided that keeping your promise to him wasn't for you?'

'I—I thought I should have a house or an apartment to look after, and that when he wasn't working, we should do things together—go out, play games, swim. Or I might have taken a job. After all, it's very usual in England for wives to work nowadays,' she argued to the implacable mask of Vicente's face, 'and I've been a working girl all my life. In fact, I've wondered whether that was why my father made me promise to write to you. With his own foundry failing, he may have hoped you would find me a job in yours. But of course I don't know about that,' she finished lamely.

'Indeed?' enquired Vicente judicially. 'It's news to me that he had any such hope. And did you entertain it too?'

'It didn't occur to me. I just kept my promise to him to write to you. For the sake of my grandfather's association with yours, I thought.'

'And if it had occurred to you, when I innocently sent Benno into your clutches, you probably saw marriage to him as an easier way of earning a meal ticket than getting a job with Crystos? And only later got a conscience or cold feet about marrying him, and ran out?'

Tania could only stare in speechless impotence to fight back. She could tell him the truth of why she had escaped from Benno, but that would be to foil her plan to find out how far he himself was implicated in Benno's treachery against her father.

And as the chance of revenge which she had bought with her marriage to him was more important than pleading her case, she remained silent, riding the insult with difficulty.

For the moment her one impulse was to escape the dark mockery of his expression as he waited for the answer he wasn't going to get. But she couldn't even escape him. She was in bed, imprisoned by the tray across her knees, and she knew he had interpreted her desperate glance across to her dressing-room when he stood up, relieved her of the tray and said, 'Oh no! Not the melodrama of a locked door, please! In fact, no locked doors ever—you understand? Also, Signora Vicente Massimo is not to be seen to work for her living in her husband's firm or anywhere else. Understand that too. It is an order.'

On his way out of the room he turned at the door. 'Meanwhile, the fulfilled smile of a bride of a night—for Madrigna's benefit, please.' His tone made that an order too.

It did not take Tania long to realise how mistaken she had been in supposing that her everyday exchanges with Vicente would afford her enough sidelights on his work to give her a line on what use, if any, he meant to make of her father's stolen papers. Her mind had argued, and still did, that he wouldn't have denied their existence if he hadn't had some sinister purpose with regard to them. She could be wrong. But Benno must have learned something from them which she didn't know, and in dealing with Benno's affairs Vicente could have realised its value too. But she was to find that he brought none of his problems or plans back to the Villa for discussion, even with Fabia. He frequently dealt with them there in his study, but he did not talk about them. He was well aware of Tania's own knowledge of the glass industry, but he chose to ignore it completely. Perhaps further to discourage her idea that Crystos might have a use for her, or perhaps from the common chauvinism that the male's working interests weren't for sharing with wives.

Whichever it was, or something else again, she was gradually to learn that in other spheres than this of his work, Vicente was going to withhold his confidence from her, debar her from any but a physical knowledge of him as a man, and allow himself to show no more than a physical interest in her. That was the measurement of his punishment of her, she supposed—punishment for a crime of which she wasn't guilty.

She would not have been a woman if his smoke-screen had not intrigued her; she would not have been his enemy if she had not looked for a chink in his armour through which she might inflict a hurt. His very indifference made her all the more acutely aware of him, aware as she had never been of any other man. Curiosity and speculation about him dominated her thoughts. Resentment of his treatment of her came to a head one night after she had played hostess to half a dozen business colleagues and competitors at dinner.

Vicente introduced her to each of them and they made polite conversation with her over their aperitifs. It was her first experience of hostessship where she was the only woman, but she had the impression that her guests were more embarrassed by her than she was by them.

They congratulated her on her Italian, but didn't wait to hear that from childhood it had been her second language at home. They asked how she liked Venice, had she relatives in Italy, had Vicente yet taken her to Rome? But she felt that the English girl whom Vicente had married within a few weeks of her tragic loss of her fiancé, and his brother, was a curiosity to whom they had difficulty in relating, and that they were only too glad to revert to talking business shop with Vicente and each other.

She was irritated. Vicente should have told them something of her background, so that they could have drawn her into their technical talk of glass if they chose. At home her father and his few associates had regarded her as equally know-ledgeable as they. But these grandees of the world of crystal ignored her, except for an occasional smiled apology for talking across her, and when she did throw in a remark which she knew made a technical point, it was uncanny how swiftly Vicente broke in to turn the discussion aside to something else. If it were possible he could already suspect her of spying in his camp, he couldn't have been more watchful of what she might say or hear!

When she left them to their liqueurs and brandy, she supposed they would join her later in the *salotto*. But Vicente, escorting her to the door as the others came to their feet and bowed, whispered that they might decide to stay on at the table and later might break up from there. Not knowing whether he expected her to reappear or not, she waited in the *salotto* for a long time and then decided to go to bed. Fabia, having handed over to Tania duties which she had hitherto done for Vicente, had already gone.

Very soon after reaching her room Tania had not begun to undress when movement and talk in the hall showed that the party was over. By that time her resentment was not to be contained, and she was spoiling for a verbal fight when Vicente came upstairs.

He discarded the cigar he had been smoking when he entered the room and went to sit on the other end of the long dressing stool on which she sat. So, he facing outward and she to her mirror, they were in the typical love-seat position, shoulder to shoulder. Speaking across his, he said, 'Wise of you not to wait. We might have been much later than this.'

She answered via the mirror, 'I don't know why I had to be there at all. For all anyone noticed me, I might have been invisible!'

His brows went up. 'Piqued?' he asked. 'You were there as my wife and the natural hostess to my guests. Would you rather I had despatched you to your room with your dinner on a tray? As for your being invisible, it seemed to me that you attracted enough eye-attention to do me credit, and, I'd have thought, enough to satisfy you.' As he spoke his glance travelled over her in appraisal of her slim bare shoulders and the camisole top and the long, narrow wrist-pointed sleeves of her black dinner-dress. 'Thank God, you have taste,' he added.

Tania ignored the compliment. 'I'm not talking about the kind of ogling men save for Miss World contests,' she snapped. 'I mean that no one noticed me as a person, or wanted to listen to a word I tried to say. Anyway, haven't your friends any wives or girl-friends who could have kept me company in being ignored?'

'Wives and girl-friends weren't invited. It wasn't that kind of a party,' he pointed out. As if the subject were entirely secondary to the business of preparing for bed, he shrugged out his jacket and stood, pulling loose his tie. '*You* were there for the reason I've stated—only in the role of an attractive figurehead, no more.'

That added fuel to Tania's temper. 'But since, being who I am, I understood a good deal of what you were discussing, might you not have let me join in?' she urged.

'Calling on your experience of your father's small-time concern? I doubt if you could have contributed much that would be of value to us,' he said.

'I could at least have asked some questions, and you could have answered them.'

'With spare time on our hands, and always supposing there was anything to be gained by our acting as guides to enthusiastic amateurs in the crystal industry, no doubt,' he agreed blandly.

Of course, if he were guilty of coveting and stealing any trade secret on which her father might have lighted, he *would* try to belittle any experience she or Reggio Torre had had! she thought in sour triumph. 'And is that why you refused to entertain any idea of giving me a job in the firm—because I'm just an enthusiastic amateur in your eyes?' she demanded.

'It is not,' he denied. 'It is because, as I told you, the wife of the head of the Massimo line does not work as a paid employee—at any time or anywhere. I thought I made that clear.'

'You did,' she agreed. 'Also, it seems to me that a Massimo wife has duties, but no rights of her own.'

He was standing behind her now. '*Privileges* and duties,' he corrected, addressing her reflection in the mirror.

'Privileges—such as?' she flashed back to his.

'Principally of being chosen for a Massimo wife,' he said.

At the sheer arrogance of that Tania gasped, totally at a loss for retort. For a long moment they stared in hostile silence at each other's images. Then Vicente's hands which had rested on her shoulders, slid down her arms to her hands, knotted together in her lap.

'*Privileges*,' he emphasised again. And then,

'Come to bed.'

How could he? How *could* he think so venom-laden a quarrel could be resolved so? 'No!' she almost shouted in open revolt. '*No!*'

'No? What choice otherwise have you?'

'I can—I can use the bed in your room,' she declared wildly.

'As you please—afterwards. In the meantime, may I remind you of "duties"? Come, if you don't mean to get undressed, I must do it for you.'

She stood reluctantly and pulled the back-zip of her gown. It slid down over her hips with a silky rustle and lay, a black pool, about her feet. After that she made no further move. Vicente waited. At last she kicked free of the dress and picked it up. 'You could at least make privacy one of my supposed privileges,' she snapped at him.

'Very well.' Taking the jacket and tie he had already discarded, he left her to go to his dressing-room. She remained standing where she was and had done no more towards undressing herself when he returned. He came across the room to face her. 'Of all the least becoming attitudes in an adult woman is a nursery-type defiance,' he remarked. 'Just now, what do you hope to gain by it when there's only—this, and—this—' as he spoke his finger and thumb snapped contemptuously at her bra and panties—'between me and what I asked of you and intend to have?'

'You can't possibly want to—in the mood you're in; in the mood you must know *I* am!' she protested. 'It—it's indecent . . . animal! Resenting

you as I do tonight, I can't even *pretend* to want
you near me . . . touching me—I *can't*!'

'Shall we see?'

She recognised the quiet question for the in-
exorable command it was as he pushed the straps
of her bra from her shoulders and waited for her
to deal with the rest. Then he carried her over to
the bed, and whether or not he was having to act
the part which she had warned him she couldn't,
he became the lover, expertly wooing and seducing as always in the few times he had taken her
since their consummation. And as always, even
this time of her sore spirit's rebellion, her dis-
obedient body, compliant at first, then roused to
an almost savage need to take and to give, went to
meet his in a pulsing desire which, believing it
when she had said it, she had sworn to him she
could neither feel nor feign.

She hadn't had to pretend. They were admitted
enemies, each with warring motives. But by some
curious chemistry, his body had magic for her,
and when he left her, she knew that he took with
him the triumph of knowing it as well as she did.
How would he use it?

'Nursery-type defiance' was a phrase which
stayed to rankle. To be labelled as a naughty child
for expecting a wife's reserves and privacies to be
respected was more than Tania's pride could take
without revolt. Vicente should learn that she
could register defiance in other directions, she
resolved, giving deeper thought to a plan already

half formed in her mind.

Vicente's dismissal of her experience as puny proved that he had no intention of sharing any side of his work with her. Yet without some insight into methods and developments at Crystos in competition with the other Venetian glass foundries, she couldn't hope for a clue to whatever he or Benno might have learned to the advantage of Crystos. When she had first come to Venice, Benno at least had shown her round the foundry on the lagoon island of San Paolo, and had taken her to the elegant Crystos sales showrooms on the Piazza San Marco. But Vicente had offered her no such interest, and she would have to penetrate the industry by another way in.

Her experience in England had been in the showroom of her father's foundry, so she made a list of the same trading in Venice and visited each in turn, in search of possible vacancies for fluently English-speaking assistants behind their counters. If she managed to get acceptance at one of them, by listening and talking shop with her colleagues she might learn something she could use, and once she had been engaged, that would be a *fait accompli* which Vicente must accept or not as he pleased.

So ran her scheme—only to prove its futility in its execution.

At one or two shops she met with the blanks she knew she must expect. At one or two others her enquiry encountered the 'Don't-ring-us, we'll-ring-you' kind of polite rejection, and when one manager did show interest enough to give her an interview, he had terminated it abruptly on his asking her for her name.

'Tania Massimo.' She had given it unthinkingly, to be confounded by his sharp glance.

'Massimo?' he had repeated. 'A relation of the Massimo family? A distant one, perhaps?' he had enquired casually enough. But before she could frame an evasive reply, she could see she had no chance with him and they had parted forthwith.

Exasperated with herself for having harboured such a half-baked idea in the first place, she realised there was no point in trying elsewhere, even if she had not almost exhausted her contacts. Her one consolation was that Vicente couldn't know how ineptly she had handled her attempt to defy him, and she took some chill comfort from that until the day, some time later, when, his tone dangerously quiet, he asked her,

'I wonder, can you tell me how one of our competitors, Societa Praccino, got the mistaken idea that someone giving this telephone number had applied for a post as a saleswoman in their city showroom? I answered the telephone myself, assured them it was impossible and checked the number with them. It was correct. So perhaps——?'

Praccino! The only one of the 'Don't-ring-us' brigade with whom she had thought it worth while to leave her number—leave it with the same idiotic confidence as she had overlooked the damning evidence of her name! Tania felt all

colour drain from her face as she met Vicente's
steely glance, realising that he had only put his
question in order to goad her into useless denial
or shameful admission. He already had the
answer.

With as much bravado as she could muster she
said, 'I think you've realised they weren't mistaken, and that they were talking about me.'

'Exactly. From the description I was given, it
was obvious, though I understand you didn't give
your name.'

'They didn't ask for it—just for a number to
ring, in case they had a vacancy later.'

'And may I ask what madness inspired your
going to look for a job as a shop assistant, when I
had expressly forbidden you to undertake paid
work of any kind?'

'I didn't consider you had the right to forbid it.
I have no house ties, no children——'

'For the moment——'

'I'm skilled. Selling glassware happens to be the
thing I do best, and though an English husband
might ask his wife not to work, he wouldn't dream
of "forbidding" her,' Tania claimed.

'And an Italian wife wouldn't dream of dis-
obeying an express order such as I gave you—
with reasons for it.'

'Yes—that it would be *beneath* a Massimo wife
to work——!'

'Also that you owe some companionship to
Madrigna, and I could have added that in Italy
today a woman who needn't work doesn't, for the

sake of those who must,' he said coldly.

'You didn't *say* that!' she accused.

'Evidently I was wrong to credit you with enough public sense to realise it. However, as a matter of interest, how did you propose to take on and do any job you were offered, without my knowledge?'

'I didn't. Obviously I couldn't. If I had obtained anything I'd have told you at once that I was taking it on.'

She could hardly have incensed him more. She saw that from the red flash of anger in his eyes before he cut the distance between them and was grasping her shoulders in a vice-like grip.

'You would have "told" me!' He shook her as easily as if she were a rag doll.

'Vicente, don't! Please——You're hurting me!'

'I mean to—if that is the only way I can make you understand that *I* do the "telling" under this roof. *You* obey.' He shook her again, then thrust her roughly from him. She stumbled, regained her balance and with an effort stilled her trembling. With no weapon but her tongue against brute force, she scorned, 'I repeat—I'd have told you, out of courtesy. And if Praccino still want me——'

She got no further. 'They don't,' he cut in. 'They understood very clearly from me that no one at all was available for their vacancy at the number you gave them.'

'And suppose I chose to contradict that?' Rash, defiant inflammatory words, but even as she uttered them she knew she despised herself for arguing on this false front. For she *hadn't* gone in search of a job merely because she was bored or felt wasted, but in the faint hope of easing her spying on him. And since she couldn't admit that as her motive, she mustn't cloak it with a spirited claim to her right to disobey him. There were fair and foul means of fighting, and surprising as the thought was, she wouldn't stoop to fighting Vicente with foul.

Did that mean she had begun to respect him as an enemy? That thought surprised her too. For once you allowed that your enemy might have the right to be as he was, you were halfway into the danger of wishing he wasn't your enemy at all . . .

As, sometimes, in the heady rapture of his body's possession of her, she had allowed herself to wish he was the man she wanted in every way of marriage, and to fantasise the belief that it was true. But in the cold dawn of reality it never had been. The sword of their enmity lay between them still.

As if he knew she had conceded victory to him, he ignored the flung defiance of her question to ask,

'How much about this hare-brained scheme does Madrigna know? Or have you been afraid she would persuade you that I ought to hear of it, so you haven't told her?'

'She knows nothing about it.' On a dying spurt of defiance Tania added, 'But I suppose you'll think it your duty to tell her?'

He shook his head. 'If I can't command any more loyalty from you than you've shown in this affair, I'd rather not publish the fact,' he said dismissingly. And recognising now that a disloyalty she had thought justifiable was at the very heart of her rebellion, Tania found herself with no retort to make.

CHAPTER FIVE

THAT defeat at Vicente's hands brought Tania up against a blank wall of frustration. How was she now to prove there was anything suspicious about the disappearance of her father's papers? *Someone* must be led to volunteer the information she needed. But who?

There was nothing to be gained by sounding Fabia, the widow of one Massimo and the step-mother of another, for she was surprisingly content to know little or nothing of her men's work. From his telephone talk, Tania had deduced that Benno's news of his 'goldmine' had been the first Pascale Fedore had heard of it. But he had been in Benno's confidence, and if he hadn't been driven by Vicente into disappearing from her scene, he might have helped her. What was more, believing the lie which Vicente had later turned into the truth, Pascale had voluntarily abandoned her. That had hurt badly, and had turned him from potential ally to enemy.

There remained only Sophia Greniere, Benno's mistress. She had been at his funeral. According to him, she had been jealous of Tania herself, and had known her by sight well enough to point her out to Pascale. She had had to swallow the hum-iliation of Benno's projected marriage, but Tania

suspected she would have exacted from him the
reason for her displacement, and he would have
placated her with promises that, because of the
'goldmine', nothing about their liaison would
have to change.

It was all speculation, of course, and Italian
mistresses might be as shut out from their lovers'
business confidence as apparently were Italian
wives. But with Sophia Greniere as the only link
to Benno's secret which Tania had, her acquaintance had to be made—somehow.

She had an apartment in a *palazzo* near the
Accademia Bridge, Tania learned from the city
telephone directory, and watched the building
from a seat in the shade of a gnarled olive tree on
several fruitless mornings, until she realised her
disadvantage if her quarry, unknown to her by
sight, should recognise her and speak to her. How,
taken off guard, was she to explain her purpose in
that secluded square?

But chance was to take a hand. When she came
into the city, Rietti would drive her to the Piazzale
Roma and either go on some domestic messages
for Fabia or wait for her in the car. On the morning that she had abandoned her vigil as useless,
when she returned to the car park he was
crouched beside a scarlet sports model in the next
slot, changing one of its wheels for a spare.

Beside him stood a young woman in a black
silk suit, its brief skirt moulded tightly to her
shapely thighs, its jacket thrust back by a beringed
fist on one hip. Over her other arm was slung a

huge crocodile bag. Her black hair was caught in a heavy knot behind a narrow, sleek head and small, madonna-fine features. Bent to the chauffeur, she was making encouraging noises and murmuring her thanks; the typical damsel in distress with no lack of a knight errant, Tania thought amusedly as she approached.

Rietti had stood up, dealt with the discarded wheel and the tools he had used, dusted down his hands and was bowing his refusal of the lire notes being offered to him.

'*Grazie, no, signora.*' His figure stiffened in his uniform.

'But I insist! So very kind!' The voice was low, with a huskiness, the smile persuasive. At sight of Tania, 'Your man, *signora*—he has changed my wheel after a puncture, but he refuses——' The woman broke off, perfect teeth set in her lower lip as she stared. 'But I know you, *signora!*' she said, her smile widening as she held out her hand.

She could have been any one of the family's friends, but she was so striking a figure that Tania knew they hadn't met. She took the hand, its clasp limply formal. 'I'm afraid you are ahead of me, *signora*. I don't think I know you,' she said.

'Of course not—we haven't met!' The stranger fingered the notes again, but put them away in the capacious bag when she saw that Rietti was now rigid in his driving seat. She turned again to Tania at the very instant at which Tania's sixth sense registered, '*Sophia Greniere!*' and introduced herself, 'My name is Greniere, Sophia

Greniere, and I only know you through having seen you once with my very good friend, Benno Massimo, and again at his *tragic* funeral. You wouldn't have seen me, of course, and I couldn't intrude—*Cara mia*, I was so sorry!' The dark eyes beneath the delicately etched brows could have been melting in genuine sympathy if Tania hadn't remembered that, according to Benno, their owner had been 'insane with jealousy' of herself. As it was, though repelled, she couldn't afford to show it.

It was strange, she thought. In laying her plans, she had expected that if she ever made Sophia's acquaintance, she would have had to surmount and somehow disarm her obstruction and hostility. Yet here Sophia was, all pseudo-compassion, offering herself as sacrificial victim. Why?

Tania murmured thinly, 'Thank you. There were so many people at the funeral——'

'Of course. And naturally, only the family's intimates and relatives received. But you can't know how much I've wanted to offer you my sympathy; nor, when I heard you were to marry Vicente Massimo, how I wished I could tell you how sure I was that it was just what Benno himself would have wanted for you—that his brother should take his place!'

Tania cringed inwardly at the insincerity of that. 'Do you think so?' she asked. 'But did you know Benno well enough to be able to say that?'

Sophia's smile was slightly pitying. 'Oh, *very* well,' she claimed. 'We were certainly close enough, I think, to entitle me to speak for him, though after he was engaged to you I couldn't allow him to see me again. It wouldn't have been fair to you.'

(Liar, thought Tania. He was on his way to you, racing to tell you that I had escaped him, on the night that he was killed.) Aloud she said, with an insincerity of her own, 'That was generous of you, *signora*. But I'm surprised he didn't mention you to me, and he never did.'

Again the patronising smile. 'Ah, he may have thought you might be jealous!'

(And he knew you *were*!) Tania was thinking that even if Benno hadn't admitted Sophia's jealousy to Pascale, she could have read it in the other woman's every glance, every word. Jealous still, though Benno was dead? Jealous of what? Tania did not for a moment believe she had really wanted to offer condolence, but she had chosen to prolong their encounter for some reason, and as that suited Tania's own purpose, she went along with it.

'If he had ever introduced us, I think I might have been jealous of your intimacy with him,' she said, and watched Sophia preen on the implied flattery before continuing, 'So perhaps you are right, and that was why he didn't ever invite you to the Villa after he brought me there. He didn't want me to feel—eclipsed.'

Sophia's smile vanished. Her tone aloof, 'I have never visited at the Villa Massimo,' she said. 'Not that there was any reason why not, except that Benno preferred we should keep our friendship private, to ourselves. While it lasted—that is, until he fell in love with you—it was sweeter that way.'

Tania said meaningly, 'I see. I—understand.'

'I am glad. I hoped you might.' Sophia added more briskly, 'But now that it is sadly all over for both of us, couldn't we know each other a little better, and don't you think I ought now to offer my sympathy to Signora Massimo and to your husband? It would be a friendly gesture on my part, perhaps?'

'Perhaps,' Tania agreed. 'Though if they knew nothing about your intimacy with Benno——?' She left the question in the air.

'I have nothing to hide,' Sophia declared. 'And you would introduce me merely as an acquaintance of Benno's whom you had met by chance, would you not?'

Tania thought she saw light. For some reason Sophia wanted an entrée to the Villa. While she had been Benno's mistress, either she wasn't known or hadn't been welcome there, and now she saw her way in by means of Tania's introduction. But useful as she herself hoped to find her, Tania was not anxious to sponsor her at the Villa. If either Fabia or Vicente had ever heard her name linked with Benno's, their reception of her could be quite unpredictable, and Tania needed to feel her way on that one.

'I'm afraid, even after all this time, Signora Massimo still regards herself as being in mourning for Benno, and she only sees her very closest friends,' she told Sophia, and saw her eager eyes cloud.

'But you will mention that we have met?' Sophia urged, 'and you must come to my apartment. Quite soon. We must remember Benno together——' Delving into her bag, she produced a card and a gold Biro. Of the latter she explained to Tania, 'One of my last gifts from Benno before he left me for you,' and wrote on the card. 'My address and telephone number. I shall invite you, and you must come, and later I shall give a party for you and Vicente. For in Venice today he is a man one cannot afford not to *know*!'

And with what purpose in your mind, if not to make sure you are on the scene when he exploits the scheme Benno claimed to have stolen from my father? Tania's suspicious mind questioned after they had parted. Nothing about Sophia, neither her car nor her chic nor her fashionable address, evidenced that she was short of money since Benno died, but she was probably not averse to basking in the sunshine of any added fame to come for Crystos. For that she needed to penetrate the Massimo camp, and as to that, *over my dead body*, Tania determined, surprised to find herself on Vicente's side for once, guarding him and his affairs from a harpy like Sophia Greniere.

She did not want to mention their meeting at the Villa, but saw that she must before Sophia issued her promised (threatened?) invitation. Fabia repeated the name vaguely, murmured, 'Benno had many women friends before he met you, *cara*,' and plainly didn't identify Sophia as one of them. Vicente's reaction was noncommittal. He listened to Tania's account of their chance meeting, but if he had heard Sophia Greniere's name linked to Benno's, and Tania suspected he had, he was not admitting it. Having been at such cruel pains to convince her that Benno had died for love of her, he couldn't bring himself to allow that Benno had feet of clay, Tania thought bitterly. He was determined she should work through her punishment.

He had heard of Signora Greniere by name, he said. How had she recognised Tania?

'She was at Benno's funeral and had seen me there. She wondered if she ought to call and offer Madrigna her sympathy,' Tania told him.

'She could better have done that when everyone else did—at the time of his death. I doubt if Madrigna will care to be bothered with her now. Did you encourage her to come?'

'No more than was polite, I think. I told her Madrigna sees very few people, but I promised to tell you both I had met her. She wants me to visit her at her apartment on Campo San Vidal.'

'With Benno as the bond between you? How well does she claim to have known him?'

'*Very* well at one time, I believe,' Tania offered as a lead to find out how much Vicente really knew about Benno and Sophia.

'Very well?' he echoed sharply. 'Does that mean you suspect Benno of deceiving you? That you think La Greniere may have been your rival? If so, you are quite wrong. He adored you. But do you?' he urged.

Tania, however, having kept Benno's guilty secret for so long, was not ready yet to show her hand to Vicente. 'If I did, do you suppose I should want to see any more than I need of Signora Greniere, or want you and Madrigna to know her?' she parried, adding, 'After all, even before you married me, I wasn't allowed so many friends that I feel inclined to turn one down now.'

She wanted him to know she was referring to Pascale, but if he did he gave no sign of it. He agreed, 'You make your point,' and that was all.

He left her once again stabbed by the guilt of having used falsities as her weapons against him. For just as she hadn't really wanted a job in a crystal showroom, so she didn't want Sophia as a friend, but only for such use as she might be towards confounding him and Benno. The cynics might argue that all was fair in love and war. But in the war with Vicente Massimo she would have liked the pride of knowing she fought him with clean hands. And twice now they hadn't been.

If Sophia called her, she would accept an invitation for herself, she decided, leaving Vicente and Fabia to keep Sophia at arms' length if they wished. But evidently Sophia had resolved to take a short cut into the Massimo circle, for one Sunday afternoon she was shown into the garden where Fabia and Tania were sitting, and Vicente was in the pool.

She came across the lawn, both hands outstretched to Fabia, urging her not to get up. Her smile gathered Tania in as she told Fabia, 'I am Sophia Greniere. You will have heard how we—your daughter-in-law and I—met by chance the other day, and I know you are going to forgive me for intruding on you to offer you my sympathy in your loss, *signora*. I am late with it, I know, but until Signora Vicente told me I should be welcome as a friend of Benno's, I hardly liked to—you will understand?'

Fabia slowly removed her sunglasses and offered her hand. 'Yes, Tania mentioned you to us, *signora*. You knew Benno well?'

'Well enough for me to have valued his friend-ship a great deal,' Sophia replied.

'So? I am glad, though I wonder he never brought you to see us?' Fabia queried.

How was Benno's mistress going to answer that one? Tania wondered. But Sophia was equal to it. Her faint smile as modest as her words were self-belittling, she said, 'Ah, but we were never on such terms as I could allow him to bring me to you as more than a mere friend. Never, that is, in the way he brought Tania here to you—as his lovely English sweetheart whom he was going to marry.' She paused. 'I was not free, you see. I have a husband living. So how could I permit Benno any more than the warm friendship which I admit I returned, but on which I could never let him *presume* at any time!'

'I should have thought he ought still to have introduced you to us as a dear friend,' Fabia puzzled. But before Sophia had to counter that, Vicente, his towel careless across his shoulders, his magnificent torso and legs glistening wetly, came over from the pool.

As always at sight of his body, Tania experienced a thrill that was all sensual. There was nothing of her heart in it, she told herself. How could there be? Her pulse would quicken in the same admiration of a piece of nude male sculpture, wouldn't it? Yet now, as always happened, her fingers were a-leap to touch the warmth of living flesh, trace the line of muscle and bone, and linger . . . That was to 'know' a body in the way Nature intended. As Vicente's cynicism had said, she had only her own purpose to serve. She took no count of the heart's need of the love and tenderness and sharing which marriage should be. So Vicente and Tania Massimo weren't cheating Nature. They were only cheating themselves.

She would have liked to swim with him, but she rarely did. His daily habit was a routine dive and thirty lengths, as ordered an exercise as everything else he did, usually taken before he went to his office, when he didn't suggest she should join him. And as she saw swimming as a pleasure, not a discipline, she did not invite herself.

Fabia introduced him to Sophia, who explained herself in much the same terms as she had to Fabia. He asked no probing questions about her relationship with Benno, making Tania wonder again whether he knew more about it than he would admit. His manner was as politely formal as Fabia's. He excused his undress and was about to go to change when Sophia sighed a wistful, 'How lucky you are to have a pool! There is nothing at the Palazzo Cielo where I live, and if I want to swim, I have to be obliged to friends. The Contis and the Abruzzis are very good, but——'

It was so broad a hint that Fabia, the perfect hostess, could not ignore it. She exclaimed, 'But what a pity you didn't know we had one. Another time you must come prepared, *signora*——'

'Sophia, *please*!'

Fabia inclined her head. 'Thank you.' She continued, 'Or why not now? Tania, you have a suit, a bikini thing you could lend to—Sophia, perhaps?'

'Oh no!' Sophia shrank from the suggestion. Then, again wistfully, 'Well, I should so enjoy it! And you, Tania—I may call you Tania?—will join me? And——' she looked a long way up into Vicente's face—'you too, *signore*?'

'Of course they both will,' Fabia assured her briskly. 'You will all swim, and I shall order the English tea which Tania has taught us to enjoy. Tania, you can help our friend, I am sure?'

Tania took Sophia to her room and was able to provide either a spare one-piece or a white bikini. Sophia chose the bikini and with astonishingly few lithe contortions was out of her clothes and into it, smoothing it over satin-smooth bronzed hips before the mirror. She unpinned her great swathe of hair and shook it loose, cloakwise, over her shoulders.

'Aren't you going to plait it?' Tania asked.

'No, I never do. I like it to trail like a mermaid's, and Benno always loved to see it loose,' Sophia claimed, leaving Tania to wonder, as she donned the rejected ruched blue one-piece and plaited her own hair, whether that sample of mischief had been deliberate or unconscious on Sophia's part, and why, whichever it was, it couldn't hurt her any longer. She was surprised to find herself the more irked by Vicente's willingness to obey his stepmother and to wait to swim again with her and · Sophia, when he wouldn't have invited her alone.

In the water Sophia was indeed mermaid-like. The diving board was not high, but she dived with controlled grace from it, cavorting and twisting and swimming underwater to come up beside Tania, catching her round the waist, or attempting to duck Vicente, always without success.

She challenged him to race her and laughingly accused him of cheating when he easily outstripped her. Tania pottered about, porpoise-diving and doing the leisurely crawl which relaxed her and gave her most pleasure. Sophia climbed out to sit on the poolside, pedalling long slim feet in the water as she called dares to Vicente which he executed with ease.

Then she called, 'You must do a double dive—with your wife!'

Tania, who had come over to cling to the side,

shook her head. 'I've never done one.'

'There has to be a first time!'

'Not with an audience.' Tania really meant, 'Not helping Vicente to let me make a fool of myself in front of you.' She swam away.

Sophia scrambled to her feet and went over to the board. 'Then Vicente'—(he had been 'Vicente' since her first dive into the pool)—'shall do one with me,' she announced, and beckoned to him.

She stood in front of him at the edge of the board, their four arms at full stretch upward, as one pair. But suddenly Sophia dropped hers, and Tania saw Vicente's lips question, 'What?'

She had turned to face him. 'It is not exciting, that,' she said. 'This is better. I shall do a backward dive. Come——'

Heels now over the edge of the board, she drew him to her, aligned her body to the contours of his, breast to breast, hip to hip, thigh to thigh, in an erotic pose at which Tania did not want to look. Their arms went up, fingers linked, then they dived as one body—perfectly. Sophia came up laughing, a hand under the sweep of her hair. 'Again?' she invited Vicente, but he was climbing out of the pool.

'I never tempt fate. A second performance mightn't be so spectacular,' he said.

'Chicken!' she pouted at him, and stayed in the pool which she now had to herself. Head bent, Tania was using her towel on her legs, and Vicente had started for the house when Sophia called faintly, 'Tania! Vicente! Help me——' and lifted an arm ineptly from the water.

Vicente was back in a flash and across the pool to her. He turned her on her back and towed her to the shallow end, where he lifted her bodily on to the grass and bent over her. 'What was it?' he asked.

'My right leg, down to my ankle. A hideous pain—cramp, I think. I've never had it before.'

He passed his hand from her knee to her ankle. 'I can't feel any sinew tension. Try to bend your foot up at the ankle.'

She looked up at him appealingly. 'I—can't!'

'Try.'

Gingerly, grimacing, Sophia flexed her ankle. The foot responded, moved normally from side to side, and she clucked, 'Tch!' in triumph. 'It's better, the pain has gone!'

'Good,' said Vicente. 'It does.'

'But supposing you hadn't been here? Supposing I had been swimming alone?' she appealed.

'If you are liable to attacks of cramp, I hope you never do.'

'I told you, this was the first time. But if you say so, I'll promise not to,' she told him, and signalling for his hand to help her up, in one lithe movement was standing at his side. She swung his hand as they moved towards the tea-table, and it was at that moment that Tania, already suspicious of a 'cramp' which shouldn't have caused an expert swimmer like Sophia to panic, realised she was hot with jealousy of Benno's mistress. And it was not a throwback to the pain of Benno's rejection of herself; it was a jealousy of Sophia's monopoly and easy manipulation of Vicente's attention.

She did not know which would rankle with her the longer—the memory of their bodies aligned in one perfect whole, or the memory of his willing play with Sophia as he had never played with her. They both hurt equally now. She was jealous of Vicente as she would be of a lover, and that was a weakness she couldn't afford.

A fortnight later, as she dressed for Sophia's party, Tania was wondering at Vicente's ready acceptance of the invitation, issued before Sophia had left that afternoon.

He had been critical of Tania's scraped acquaintance with her, but in a couple of hours he had allowed her to work on him much the same charm as had enslaved Benno, Tania's resentment noted. If their association ripened, how long might it be before he was adding Sophia to his experience of women at which Fabia had hinted? Tania could imagine the calculated discretion he would bring to such an affair; the public image of his marriage that was no marriage would be kept above suspicion. The thought made her writhe.

Between that first afternoon and tonight Sophia had made no further overtures to herself, so that she was no nearer to her goal, and she didn't hope for anything from tonight's affair. She was attending it at Vicente's near-royal command that they both should, making of it a duty he didn't expect her to dispute. He invited himself to her bed with much the same assumption . . .

He moored the launch at the Accademia Bridge and they walked the short distance to the Palazzo Cielo. It was only dusk as yet and the Grand Canal traffic was still busy, the craft all lit, and the lamps on the mooring stanchions and the quays criss-crossing their reflected paths across the water. The air was still and warm; a single star had ventured out and a slender moon hung in the sky. It was so typical a Venetian scene that Tania thought of all the painters who had sought to capture its magic, and of the thousands of lovers who had wandered and dreamed and kissed there on just such an enchanted night, under just such a sky.

She had been one of them for the brief time she had trusted Benno, and if she allowed herself any sentimentality in front of Vicente, she might have voiced her thoughts and drawn his attention to the strolling entwined boys and girls who were the present threads in the age-old pattern of love her imagination had conjured.

For a moment or two she stood, absorbing and storing beauty. Vicente halted beside her. 'What is it?' he asked.

She weakened. She had to express something of her feelings for once. 'It's all so beautiful that I'm envying everyone who can paint or sculpt or write, and so be able to recall it whenever they want to.' She turned to him impulsively. 'Do you understand? Have you ever felt like that?'

He began to walk on. 'I don't have to recall it. It is my city,' he said, which would have made her feel snubbed, alien, if he hadn't followed it up by suggesting, 'Perhaps we'll leave this affair early and take a trip in the launch round the lagoon. Would you enjoy that?'

Astonished at his first invitation to her purely, it seemed, for her pleasure's sake, Tania said earnestly, 'I'd love it!' But then he had to spoil it with, 'I'm surprised you haven't been taken out there at night by someone in the interests of romance.'

'I've only been to your Crystos island with Benno. Never out on the lagoon *at all*,' she emphasised, guessing he was thinking of her few meetings with Pascale, whom he had forced to abandon her.

Light streamed, and a cacophony of noise chattered from Sophia's first floor apartment when they arrived. The building had indeed been a 'palace' originally occupied by one of Italy's noble first families. Its rooms were high and spacious with ornate ceilings and deeply embrasured windows looking out on to the Square below. Flowers were banked in each corner; chandeliers glittered on the kaleidoscope of shifting colour as the women moved from group to group or paired off with the men. Sophia, in a scarlet evening trouser suit, perfect for her raven colouring, embarrassed Tania by announcing to the group nearest to her—no one else was listening—that actually she was giving this party *for* the Vicente Massimos, and particularly for Signora Massimo, whom very few people had been privileged to meet, she thought, but whom she *knew* they were going to *love*.

She murmured a few introductory names, then disappeared. Tania was soon separated from Vicente and was circulated from group to group by people whose names she barely learned before she was whisked away to meet others. She had been right to expect no privacy of talk with Sophia, for Sophia, hostessing her stream of guests, was in continual demand everywhere.

Between the main salon and a further room where there was a buffet table, the personnel was always changing. While some people were still arriving, others were leaving, and Tania was wondering what Vicente had meant by 'early', when, glancing past the shoulder of the man nearest to her, she caught her breath at sight of a man in profile to her in the embrasure of a window.

He was talking and laughing with two companions.

He was Pascale Fedore.

CHAPTER SIX

PASCALE!

Pascale, whom she had liked and felt she could trust.

Pascale who, next to Sophia, might have known Benno better than anyone; who had been her first hope and might now be her last, of uncovering Benno's (and Vicente's?) duplicity.

Pascale, the one person to whom she might ultimately have confided Benno's betrayal of her.

But—Pascale, who had believed Vicente's planned lie; who had rejected her of his own accord; who had given her no chance to explain— how was he going to receive her now?

At sight of him she had started forward impulsively, to be checked by doubt before she neared him. But already she was in his view; though he was smiling when he looked up and across at her, she saw his lips draw tight as his eyes met hers, looking at her, *through* her, seeing her but choosing not to admit it, before turning back to his friends.

However, one of them had followed his glance and before she could escape was coming over to her. Though she couldn't remember his name, she knew they had met earlier in the evening, and now he was urging, 'You must meet Fedore, of Vetro

Mestiere; just back from New York and places west,' and she was clamouring faintly, 'I—My husband—We were just leaving—' until she was face to face with Pascale and he had no choice but to acknowledge her. He took her hand and bent over it. 'Thanks, Gordoni, for the privilege, but Signora Massimo and I have met before,' he said with a chilling formality quite foreign to him.

If the meeting hadn't been forced on him he would have continued to cut her, she knew. But given this chance, she had to make her eyes plead with him to allow her to explain, if not to justify. She looked nervously over her shoulder lest Vicente should come to find her before she could speak alone to Pascale. The third man had already excused himself and moved away, and the one named Gordoni asked Pascale, 'That must have been before you went abroad this time?' to be told shortly, 'Yes, before the Signora's marriage.' Upon which he said, 'Well, I'll leave you to get re-acquainted,' and left to follow his friend.

Tania at once stepped into the deep shadow cast by the window recess, facing outward, so that she could watch for Vicente's approach if and when he came. After a moment's hesitation, when she feared he too was going to walk away, Pascale turned to face her, and then, for all the urgent things she had to say to him, nothing came to her tongue but an utterly time-wasting, 'I didn't expect to see you here. I—we—hadn't heard you were back.'

Pascale rasped, 'Why should you have heard?

What difference would it have made if you had?'
He added savagely, 'I'll tell you this, *Signora
Massimo*, if I had known you were to be here, *I*
shouldn't have been! But you didn't even know
Sophia Greniere then. So how?'

'I met her by chance and she recognised me,
and she invited herself to the Villa. But Pascale,
listen—*please*'—Tania laid a hand on his arm—
'I've got to talk to you, and I haven't the time.
I've got to explain, and you have too. You could
have kept our last date; you could have given me
a hearing——!'

'What need, when I'd heard it all?'

'But you hadn't, you hadn't! It wasn't true.'

'Not *true*? That you are married to Vicente
Massimo is all a huge mistake?'

'No, no—of course we're married. But he lied
to you about it when he——' Tania checked and
tightened her grip on his arm as she caught sight
of Vicente at the far end of the long room.
Breathlessly, 'He's coming to look for me. We're
leaving. *But I must see you*. Where could we meet
one day? In the city?'

'Very well.' Her need and her urgency must
have reached him at last, for he said quickly,
'Where and when? Where do you know? The
foyer of the Danieli?'

She shook her head. 'No—it's too public.
Everyone goes there.' She thought for a moment.
'There's a tiny public garden near the Gritti
Palace, with seats. There—at eleven tomorrow?'

'Very well.'

She knew just when Vicente saw her, and as she couldn't hide that she was with Pascale, she expected him to come over to them. Instead, with a false air of patience, he waited for her out on the floor, as if prepared to give her all the time she needed to break up a guilty assignation. It was his subtle way of underlining his displeasure.

Under his breath Pascale muttered, 'He is not going to ignore *me*!', but 'No, please. Don't make trouble,' she begged him, and went to join Vicente.

'Are we going now?' she asked the dark storm of his face.

'Yes. Get your cloak.'

'I didn't bring one. But I must take my leave of Sophia.'

'I've done that for us both.' His hand beneath her elbow was that of a gaoler's, and their progress across the Square and to the mooring bay was conducted in a punitive silence. Minute by minute Tania's ire was rising—what right had he to treat her like a naughty child?—but as he handed her into the launch she made a bid for normality.

'If I'd known we were going out on the lagoon, I suppose I ought to have brought a wrap,' she said.

Vicente didn't reply until he had switched on and steered out into the stream. 'You won't need one. You aren't going anywhere tonight but home,' he told her.

'I see. No treat, and bread-and-water for my supper?' she flashed.

He shrugged. 'No question of nursery treats or punishments. Merely that I find I've little inclination for a pleasure cruise in the role of a complaisant husband, and I shouldn't think that, with your romantic sights elsewhere, you would enjoy it either. Another time, perhaps, when we are more in accord.'

'If I behave myself!' When he did not reply to that she sat low in her seat, hunched into her shoulders, determined he shouldn't tempt her to another word for the rest of the journey.

He didn't tempt her. They picked up the car on Roma and drove to the Villa in silence. There he said, 'Wait for me,' when he went to put away the car, and though she would have liked to defy him by going to bed, locking her door and forcing him to sleep in his dressing-room, she waited.

When he came to join her in the *salotto* he began, 'Well, this happy reunion with the boy-friend—was it by pure chance, or had it been planned?'

'Planned? Of course not! We've had no contact since he left Venice. *You* saw to that,' she reminded him.

Vicente agreed blandly, 'Adequately, I thought—making the rejection of the affair come from him——'

'It was *never* an affair!'

'And I had no intention it should become one beyond a point I could allow. However, are you sure Sophia Greniere hadn't slipped a hint that she had invited Fedore to her party and that he would be there?'

'I doubt if she knows Pascale and I were ever acquainted,' Tania said dully.

'And so it was a chance encounter, with the initiative coming from you?'

'No!' she lied.

'Oh, come—he wasn't at all welcoming at first sight of you, and you had to call the tune, I think?' Vicente parried.

She realised then that he must have been watching her for longer than she thought and had seen her impulsive move towards Pascale.

She said, 'I'm not ashamed of being glad to see him. He was my *friend*!'

'And no doubt the snatched meeting had all the attraction of clandestinity?'

'If you saw me go to meet him, you'll know we had only a few minutes together before you were waiting for me.'

'Exactly. Only long enough to make a date for a longer and less public a session? When and where?'

She could have lied again, but knew she wasn't proof against his intuition. 'You have no right to ask me,' she defended.

'No *right*?' He moved across to her, his dark gaze a threat. 'My dear, you must think of a better reason than that for refusing to tell me! You arrange a rendezvous with your fancy man, and have the effrontery to deny me the right to question you about it! Come—' he took her roughly by the shoulder—'time and place, if you please.'

Unable to resist the empty defiance, 'I *don't* please,' she said.

'So!' Vicente released her. 'Then we must see you don't leave the house to go anywhere unaccompanied, mustn't we?' he suggested.

'That's ridiculous—you can't imprison me!'

His tone smooth, he agreed, 'Ah, I hoped you would agree to spare me the melodrama of that. And so—I'm waiting?'

She gave in. 'Very well—though how much guilt you can make of a date for a talk in a public garden in mid-morning, I'd be glad to hear,' she said.

'Innocent daylight chit-chat, hm? But the French have a saying, "It's the first step which counts", and so, which garden and which morning?'

'Tomorrow; a little garden near the Gritti—I don't know its name.'

'At your suggestion or his?'

'Mine.'

'M'm—a pity to have seemed so eager, and then not to be there,' Vicente mused almost to himself.

'You mean you're forbidding me to go?'

He didn't answer. Instead he went round the big room, turning out lights, then to the door, and short of staying where she was in the dark, Tania had to follow him. At the door he paused to say meaningly, 'I deplore the necessity to "forbid". So I'm assuming that, as my wife, you are aware of the consequences of taking even the first step towards a liaison on—to be crude—the wrong side of the marriage blanket. You understand, and therefore you won't go?'

'Pascale will be expecting me,' she muttered, defeated.

'No longer than is necessary. But in case you are tempted, perhaps you need other and stronger persuasions as to who is the man in sole possession of your favours and intends to remain so. Come to bed,' he ordered, making his intention clear.

He took her that night with cold deliberation, without any attempt to rouse her to response. As he had warned, he was merely stating his dominant possessive right to her body, and to that she had no warmth of response to give.

At breakfast when Fabia reminded him that she had an appointment with her oculist that morning, Vicente said, 'Yes, and I think Tania should come with you. If you like, I'll book a table at the Danieli for luncheon, and I'll join you there, just the three of us. You did say something you had planned for the morning had fallen through, didn't you?' he added to Tania, underlining the veto he had laid down overnight.

She scorned to ask whether he had allowed Pascale to wait in vain for her at their rendezvous, or whether he had telephoned Vetro Mestiere to say that she wouldn't be there, but during the following days Pascale made no effort to contact her, and strangely she was reluctant to try for another, this time really, clandestine arrangement with him. Vicente should *not* have the chance to accuse her of that!

Though she was far from resigned to abandoning her quest for Benno's secret, it seemed that she was fated to find her way blocked. Failing Pascale, she supposed she must fall back on Sophia, and in sending her thanks for the party she added a note inviting Sophia to lunch in the city on any day she chose.

Sophia rang her enthusiastic reply. *So* charming of Tania to invite her. They hadn't had their little talk about Benno yet, had they? But as she was practically double booked for as far ahead as she could see, might she suggest instead an early evening drink at her apartment—so much cosier and more intimate for a private talk, wouldn't Tania agree? She added a suggested day which Tania accepted. Since Sophia appeared anxious to discuss Benno, it should not be too difficult to put the leading questions to which she needed answers, Tania thought.

She told Fabia where she was going, to which Fabia demurred that the Villa owed hospitality to Sophia, but was satisfied when Tania explained that Sophia had suggested the tête-à-tête herself. All the same, Tania must take Sophia some flowers, which Tania did, and was readjusting the bouquet on her arm after ringing Sophia's bell when the door was opened, not by Sophia, but by Pascale.

'Oh!' Surprise mingled with dismay jerked the exclamation from her as she fell back a step. 'Sophia said she would be alone. She didn't tell me—I didn't expect——'

'No. But come in, won't you?' Pascale stood aside for her, shut the door and took the flowers from her when she was inside. 'I'm sorry, but this seemed the only way of seeing you. Sophia isn't here and won't be. You understand?' he asked.

'No!'

'But you did want to see me? Quite badly, I guessed. Then when you didn't come that morning——'

'My husband forbade me to.'

'That's what he gave me to understand when he rang me at work and said you wouldn't be there.'

'Then he did tell you?'

'Yes, and left me in no doubt that it would be of no use my trying to make another date. I was worried for you, Tania, more than I can say. But until Sophia suggested inviting you here and lending me the apartment for an hour, I hadn't dared to get in touch with you, lest I made difficulties for you if I did.'

Tania puzzled slowly, 'You are saying that Sophia planned this? For you to be alone here, when I came?'

'Yes, and I was grateful.'

'I hadn't realised you knew her well enough for her to do you such a favour?'

'Well, I admit she has shown more interest in me since I have been back this time, but of course I've known her for a long time—through Benno.'

Since, through no plan or fault of her own, she

was here, alone with Pascale as she had wanted, Tania decided to go straight to the point of her need. She said, 'You mean—through your knowing they were lovers? Even that she was still his mistress all the time he was courting me?' and knew from the shock in Pascale's face that she was right, and Sophia had lied.

'You knew? How?' Pascale breathed.

'I overheard him talking to you on the telephone on the day he was killed. He only called you Pascale; you made yourself known to me later. But he was boasting to you about Sophia and about me, and if you can remember what he told you, you may imagine what it did to me?' Tania invited.

Slowly and accurately Pascale remembered aloud, and her slight nods confirmed every word. At the end, he asked, 'And what happened, once you knew? If he hadn't died, you were going to marry him the next week?'

'Yes. But after that, knowing I couldn't, I planned to leave the Villa that night. I wrote to tell him so and why, but though he got my letter, he didn't try to see me, but went to keep his date with Sophia, and Vicente caught me as I was leaving and forced me to wait to see Benno when he came home—which of course he never did.'

'But you told Vicente what you knew?'

She shook her head. 'No. He decided for himself I was running out on Benno, and after Benno died, I couldn't bring myself to betray him either to Vicente or his stepmother, who adored him, on no more evidence than the bit of hearsay I had. I had to have more, and that—' she hesitated—'I'm afraid was where you came in.'

'Once you knew me, you decided to use me—is that what you are saying?' Pascale asked harshly. 'You could have spared me that!'

'*Before* I knew you I meant to find you if possible, and to try. But once we were friends, I thought it was just a matter of time before I could appeal to you to help me. Only then suddenly there was no more time. You were going away, and when Vicente told you what he did, you refused to see me again.'

'Well, what did you expect? And he didn't lie. You have married him, haven't you?'

'He did lie. He hadn't even asked me then, and when he did I agreed for two reasons only—because it made Signora Massimo happy for him to take Benno's place with me, and I was determined to find out, if I could, how much he was involved in Benno's cheating of me.'

'Neither of them reason enough for tying yourself in marriage to a man you didn't love. And you didn't, did you?' Pascale appealed.

'I think I almost hated him at the time.'

'Oh, Tania, you should have waited for me!' Pascale drew up a chair beside hers and reached for her hands, bending over them.

She sighed. 'I couldn't afford to. If I had refused Vicente I couldn't have stayed on at the Villa, and I needed to, for my plan. You had believed him and had rejected me, and besides——'

Pascale looked up. 'Besides—you didn't love me any more than you loved him.' His hurt eyes met hers, then glanced away. 'All right, you don't have to spell it out. I was living on cloud nine, when all you wanted of me was my "help". Isn't that so?'

'Your friendship too. Enough of it to make you want to help me, I hoped,' she said quietly. 'I had—and still have—enough for you to feel I can ask you.'

'And you can.' He sat back, squaring his shoulders as if adjusting a load. 'That is, you can ask me, though what do you think I can tell you, that you haven't found out from Vicente by marrying him?'

'I don't know,' she sighed. 'I don't know *anything*, except that Benno told you he was marrying me because I was potentially rich without knowing it, something he could only have found out—if he really had—from the notes and papers my father left behind. He took charge of them, and Vicente dealt with *his* effects after he was killed. But when I asked Vicente about the papers, he denied there had been anything except my father's will, which I already had. Which made me wonder whether he could be in a plot to cheat me too. But as I say, I've no proof—none at all.'

Pascale said thoughtfully, 'It's very thin, and in all justice you can't implicate Vicente merely on his denial he found any papers. Benno may have destroyed them, having decided they were of no value after all.'

'Which I can't know, can I?' Tania pointed out.

'No. But what do you suspect he may have discovered which he thought made it important to marry you?'

She said again, 'I don't know. But supposing it were some new method or process my father was working on—or even had discarded as impractical? Because he was like that—impatient of any idea which didn't develop easily, or for which he never had the funds or the backing.'

'He wouldn't discuss them with you before he abandoned them?'

'Never. But that is where I hoped you could help. You are in crystal; *could* Benno have lighted on something which he saw as a goldmine?'

'It's possible,' Pascale allowed. 'As you know, glass is a craft that is centuries old, and the furnace-blown crystal isn't manufactured, it is fashioned. Not much room for change in traditional methods there. But in other departments—m'm, yes. Though if Vicente were going to help Crystos to your father's secrets, I'd have thought he would have put it on the line by now. He hasn't mentioned any breakthrough or policy change to you?'

'He never discusses his work at home, even with his stepmother.'

'And so I gather you want me to keep my ear to the ground in business circles—in case?'

'That's what I hoped,' Tania said gratefully.

'There's no other way I can find out.'

'If Benno were guilty, you would have wanted him pilloried, if he had lived, and failing him, you want the same for Vicente?'

She moved uncomfortably. ' "Pilloried" is an ugly word. You think I shouldn't pursue it?'

Pascale said, 'I know you mean to, and I'll help you. You want justice for your father. But what would it mean to your marriage if you could prove it against Vicente?'

'I don't know.' (How often she had repeated that this evening!) She looked at a future she hadn't considered. 'It would—go on, I suppose.'

'He tricked you into it!'

'No. I told you, I went into it for my own reasons. He hadn't to force me, once I decided.'

'It couldn't be——?' Pascale stopped, embarrassed, and she had to supply for him, 'No, it couldn't be annulled. There would be no cause.'

'Then it wasn't just an—arrangement between you? It was a marriage?'

She hated telling him so, but she owed him the truth. 'It was—is—marriage,' she said.

She left before Pascale expected Sophia to return, and did not let him see her to the Accademia landing stage. At parting from her he suggested that if and when he had any news for her he should ask the loan of Sophia's apartment again. But she would not have that. She had been tricked into using it this time, and admittedly she had taken advantage of it. But when Vicente had implied that she was on her honour as his wife

not to attempt to see Pascale again, she had meant
not to appeal to him, but to rely instead on whatever Sophia might be able to tell her. So she
would not make a date with him. If he had anything to tell her, he could write to her, since at
least Vicente did not censor her mail. Even that,
she knew, was to come to uneasy terms with her
conscience. Vicente would see no difference between her corresponding with Pascale and meeting him, and of course there was none. But she
had put her problem into Pascale's hands now,
and such was her obsession with proving Benno
guilty, there was no turning back.

Proving Benno's guilt? *Only* Benno's? Yes—

For the first time she openly faced a realisation
which had been in the undercurrents of her mind
for some time now. She wanted her campaign of
revenge to stop short at Benno. She didn't *want*
Vicente to be guilty too. She had begun to find it
difficult to believe he was; his forceful personality
was such that she doubted it ever had to resort to
underhand means to gain its ends. He would
always take what he wanted in face of his world,
and in this she didn't want to think of him hand-
in-hand with Benno in paltry deception.

She had doubted him to Pascale, but she hadn't
been able to answer Pascale's shrewd question
about the future of her marriage if Vicente were
guilty. Pascale might well have expected her to
retort, 'I should leave him'. But she hadn't and
couldn't, and been almost glad to assure him that
it was sealed against annulment.

Why? She caught her breath, half in wonder, half in dread, at the honest answer that she couldn't envisage a world that was not dominated for her by Vicente, by his ever-presence in her thoughts, by the magnetism of the man which had drawn her into his field of power and kept her there—though not unwillingly now.

She remembered how she had once thought she could fall in love with his hands; how unresistingly she had yielded to the demands of his body upon hers, even when she thought she hated everything he stood for in her life. Was it possible then that she *loved* him now? And if she did, while to him she was merely an object to be used for his own revenge, where was it all going to end?

Rietti had driven her in to the car-park, but not knowing how long Sophia would expect her to stay, she had sent him back, saying she would take a taxi home. When she arrived Vicente was out and Fabia hadn't returned from a quiet dinner with friends—for which Tania was thankful. She hadn't wanted to lie to either of them about her supposed tête-à-tête with Sophia . . .

The turmoil of her thoughts went with her to bed and kept her awake for a long time. She was puzzled about Sophia's part in Pascale's dilemma. Had the loan of her apartment to him been a gesture of real friendship, or, as Tania suspected, did Sophia enjoy intrigue for intrigue's sake? The thought of being under an obligation to Sophia, and that she must have known Pascale's date with herself was a clandestine one, made Tania writhe.

Did Sophia expect to be thanked? she wondered, but decided she couldn't bear any nudge-nudge, we-girls-must-stand-together response from Sophia if she attempted it. Pascale and Sophia had set up the ruse between them without consulting her, so let any due gratitude come from him. She wasn't going to let it happen again, and with nothing to link her to Sophia Greniere but their rivalry for Benno, the less contact they had in the future, the better. *She* wouldn't seek any.

It was the one firm resolve which emerged from that night of wakeful questioning and muddled thinking. She slept heavily at last and was not disturbed when Vicente came to bed, whenever that was. He was gone before she woke in the morning, and it was the measure of her weathervane state of mind that she was more frustrated than relieved by his absence.

She wanted him there in person, to see what his casual touch, the sound of his voice, his often unreadable scrutiny had done to make her feel bound to him by a new force with no less a pull than that of her late need for revenge against him. Benno still appeared as the enemy which Vicente was no longer in her thoughts of him, and she needed his physical nearness to tell her whether her imagination was playing her false in persuading her to this wishful thinking of him as a man to whom she deeply longed to be wife in every sense of the word, or whether he would still be the monster of glacial injustice he had appeared until now.

Foolish as it was to suppose she would know, simply by seeing him briefly before he left for the city, she got up quickly, only to be further frustrated by Fabia's news that he had already gone to the airport to be away for several days on a business trip, with England as part of his itinerary, Fabia believed.

Away and to England, and telling Fabia of his plans, ignoring her own right to learn of his movements! Tania had to conceal her hurt sense of affront and must have succeeded, for Fabia, noticing nothing, announced next that she really ought to 'do something' about Signora Greniere. They would give a quiet dinner party for her when Vicente returned—just themselves and one or two friends who had known Benno.

Fabia consulted her diary and chose a date. Perhaps, as it would be quite informal, Tania would like to invite Sophia when she wrote or telephoned her thanks for last evening?

Tania did not 'like', but had to refrain from saying so.

CHAPTER SEVEN

FABIA was to confess to difficulties in finding among her friends people who were free to meet Sophia. Riffling through her diary in search of names, she complained to Tania, 'Everyone I ask, mentioning Signora Greniere, seems to be entertaining guests themselves, or joining a party for the theatre, or leaving on holiday that very day. So annoying. I had planned for two congenial couples and two single men to make up our numbers, but it looks as if I may have to content myself with the three I already have—a bachelor, still unmarried because he is rather dull, I am afraid, and a married pair, not really young enough for you or our guest to find amusing. I could not have chosen a worse night if the President himself were giving a party!'

She spoke in all innocence of something which Tania suspected—that at least some of the people in the Massimo circle may have known enough of Benno's association with Sophia to be unwilling to meet her under Fabia's roof—a classic case, Tania reflected, of those most concerned being the last to hear of scandal close to home. It was plain Fabia had no inkling that Sophia's claim to mere blameless friendship with Benno was a mask. About Vicente Tania was not so sure. But if he had any doubts of Sophia's integrity, surely he would have warned Fabia against inviting her to the Villa, even if he didn't see fit to explain his veto? Fabia would not have questioned it, Tania felt certain.

She had wondered several times also that though Sophia had pretended to her that the affair had ended on Benno's engagement, she hadn't bothered to hide what its nature had been. She must have known that Tania could either let slip or deliberately pass on the unsavoury facts to Vicente or Fabia. Which seemed incredibly careless, if she wanted to be accepted by the Massimos, as Tania was convinced she did.

Exquisitely gowned in sea-green corded silk and a silver-lined shoulder cape, she was the last to arrive for the dinner party, and Fabia, busy with her other guests, asked Tania to see her to the bedroom set aside for cloaks. At the dressing-table, examining her flawless make-up, she murmured admiration of Tania's simple white ballet-length dress.

'Such perfect taste for a young bride—almost virginal! I mustn't ask whose model it is, but obviously Vicente sees that you go to the best fashion houses. You are a very lucky girl!'

'In fact, I brought it with me from England when I came,' Tania said dryly, and some reserve in her tone must have struck Sophia, for she smiled knowingly at their reflections in the mirror as she coaxed, 'Come, I believe you are annoyed at my little trick the other night! You haven't thanked me, nor praised the idea, whereas poor

Pascale, who was desperate to see you, was beside himself with gratitude. I thought you would be as pleased. But it was a happy lovers' reunion for you—yes?'

'Pascale Fedore is not my lover!' Tania denied indignantly. 'He knew Benno well, and is just a friend of mine.'

'Oh, my dear, we all say that of our little adventures. It has become a cliché which covers a great deal.' Sophia's tone was pitying. 'You had met again too briefly at my party, and Pascale was so insistent he must see you, I felt I must help him, poor boy.'

'All the same, I'd rather you hadn't done it as you did,' Tania muttered. 'It tricked me into seeing him when I was supposed to be visiting you, and I didn't like that. It made me feel— cheap.'

'Even though an earlier rendezvous you had agreed to had fallen through—or been forbidden perhaps?'

'It wasn't important—just something we hadn't talked about before he went abroad. Things I wanted to ask him—about Benno.'

'About *me* and Benno?' Sophia demanded sharply.

'Not about you and Benno,' Tania assured her patiently. 'Things I hoped Pascale could help me with—*private* things, do you mind?'

Sophia looked relieved. 'And so I must believe you—that it was business only, and that you came home able to make an amusing story of how you had found Pascale in residence, instead of me?'

'No, I didn't mention it—as it happens,' said Tania.

'Why not?' Sophia snapped.

Tania began to feel trapped. 'Because, as I've said, I thought it was a cheap trick, and Vicente and my mother-in-law might have felt the same.'

'Protecting me from their criticism? How good of you. Or—' Sophia paused—'could it have been that you would have found it difficult to explain—to Vicente in particular—the long hours it had taken you to discuss this private business with Pascale?'

'Long hours!' Tania echoed. 'I was there with him for less than one! He must have told you I had left some time before you came back.'

'Which wasn't in fact until close upon midnight, by which time Pascale wasn't there either; he had left me a note of thanks and a bouquet——'

'Flowers *I* had brought you,' Tania pointed out.

'Really? A sweet thought. And so, though you didn't tell them the tale about your evening, your people were cosily at home when you got back, awaiting your return?'

If she had been alert enough to the purpose of the question, she could have lied, Tania was to think later. But taken off guard, she said, 'No, I remember my mother-in-law was out to dinner, and I didn't see Vicente that night. He was very late home.'

'Ah——' Sophia paused, watching extravagantly manicured fingers play an imaginary scale on the surface of the dressing-table. 'So no one to whom it might be important news could know for certain that you didn't spend a very long evening with Pascale Fedore—could they?' she mused.

Tania watched the trap close, but she tried bluff. 'And who would care how long I was talking to Pascale that night?' she parried.

'Well, I'd have thought, those from whom you kept the fact of your having met him at all. For your own good reasons, no doubt, and *private* ones at that.' Sophia stood up and gave an unnecessary pat to her chignon. 'No, my dear,' she continued, 'I think you and I are on level terms now. There are matters which I have allowed you to understand about my relations with Benno, but which I prefer should not become common knowledge, and you, I feel sure, would not care to admit to your relatives that you have no proof of your *not* having been alone in my apartment with your admirer for several hours. So neither of us will tattle about the other, I think. We are in each other's pocket, as the saying goes.'

The trap was shut, but Tania beat against the bars. 'No proof?' she scorned. 'The maids will all remember I was home by eight o'clock!'

Sophia retorted, 'No doubt—if you must stoop to the evidence of domestics and if you pay them well enough. But what a humiliating scene for you—"Tell *il signore*, Luisa—or Katerina or Bella or whoever—that I was in bed and asleep by nine that night"—No, little English Tania, I think we shall both hold our tongues, do not you?'

Tania did not reply, and on her way to the door Sophia's eye caught the ornate 'M' scroll on the bedhead. 'Such a proud family, the Massimos; one of the oldest and noblest names in Italy. A *great* pity to smirch it with tales of amours and liaisons, don't you agree?' she murmured. There was still a private little smile on her lips when Tania took her into the *salotto* for Fabia to make introductions all round.

While he was away, Tania had had time to nurse her hurt that Vicente hadn't told her he was going to England, and when he had returned a few days earlier, she had reproached him with it.

'You might have known I should be interested in where you meant to go while you were there,' she told him, prepared for a curt reply which would tell her nothing she would have liked to know.

It came. 'London—naturally. And your part of the world, the Midlands. And Hull in the north,' he had said, but then, to her surprise, had shown thought for her by adding, 'It was a business trip. I couldn't take you with me, and Madrigna advised me against telling you England was on my route, in case it made you homesick.'

Tania had wished the concern for her had been his own, not prompted by Fabia, but at least he had mentioned it.

'I see,' she had said. 'But I didn't even know

you had gone away until Madrigna told me. And—' this time surprising herself by the admission—'I'm not very homesick for England now.'

He had looked at her in his searching way which might mean anything or nothing. 'You have found consolations here?' he had asked.

'For England, merely as England—yes.'

'Also for the friends you would have had there?'

'After my father died there was no one very close. Our interests had been the same, and that had seemed enough.'

He had nodded, accepting that as an answer and probing no further. But it had been the first time since their wedding night, when he had asked her whether she feared him, that his questions seemed to show he was aware she had emotions and reactions like anyone else. Such as it was, it was a breakthrough in their relationship.

Tonight, in the light of her own new awareness and value of him, she was able to watch him as she had planned—handsome, as urbane a host as Fabia was a gracious hostess—able even to draw out the stolid young man, Tertio Ravenna, who was Tania's partner at dinner. He had Sophia, for whom the party was given, on his right hand and Signora Rienzi on his left, and though at the round table the talk was mostly general, a jealousy which Tania now admitted and a resentment of Sophia which burned, noted how often her enemy managed to engage his attention for herself, creating a little island of intimacy which isolated everyone else.

They had left the table and were at the coffee and liqueurs stage in the *salotto* when mention was made of an evening carnival being held in Padua that night. 'On the Piazza del Santo, yes. Oh, couldn't we go?' Sophia enthused. 'I do so enjoy a *festa*, don't you?' she appealed to her audience.

Both Signor Rienzi and his wife shook their heads. 'Too rowdy and going on too late,' they echoed each other. Fabia smiled her indulgence of Sophia's overdone eagerness, saying, 'Not for me either, but why don't you young people go?' Her glance ranged over Sophia and Vicente and Tania and Tertio Ravenna, then back to Vicente for his verdict.

Sophia had also turned to him, sparkling. 'Say yes,' she begged, and after a bare moment's pause, to Tania's surprise and chagrin, he agreed with Sophia, 'Why not?' Not that she would have dreamed of doing so, Tania thought she knew what his response would have been, had she alone made the suggestion.

It seemed to be taken for granted that she and her partner were agreeable; also, by Sophia, that the young man had a car in which he would drive Tania. But he hadn't one; he had ridden out from Mestre on his motor-cycle, and Sophia feigned enough grace to accept Vicente's ruling that they would all travel together in his car. With scarcely a gesture of deference to Tania, she took the seat by his side, while Tania and

Tertio Ravenna sat behind.

Considering that the _festa_ was in honour of St Antony of Padua, he was noticed only by the side booths selling holy pictures and candles and souvenir bric-à-brac. For the rest, the immense arena was a fairground, garishly lighted, festooned with bunting and deafeningly noisy with celebration of the patrons' tastes.

There were wine booths and sideshows and shooting galleries and enclosures for dancing to music which couldn't be heard above the general din; and sweetmeat stalls and a Tunnel of Love and in contrast to the glare, deeply shadowed niches and corners created by the stall awnings, where courting couples giggled and kissed in the privacy of the dark.

Vicente drove slowly round the perimeter, then they left the car to walk. Inevitably, (intentionally on Sophia's part, was Tania's jealous guess) their party became divided by two, Vicente and Sophia one half of it, moving away with Sophia's hand snuggled closely under Vicente's arm. Watching them go and trying to give her attention to Tertio at the same time, Tania wondered at Vicente's apparent willingness to be so commandeered, and at what it could be that Sophia hoped to gain by blatant feminine witchery. He was married to _her_, wasn't he, Tania argued to herself, taking perverse comfort from a fact she would have given anything to deny only a few weeks ago.

She and Tertio wandered about the ground. He won an articulated green crocodile for her at a shooting gallery, and she bought the least showy thing she could find, a set of lace dinner-mats, for Fabia from the lace-making island of Burano. They drank wine, standing in the crush of a wine bar, and Tania enjoyed watching the gesticulations without which Italians seemed lost for emphasis, and which, once they were in full flow, seemed to say as much for them as their tongues.

She and Tertio returned to the car before the other two. Vicente had given Tertio a key so that they were able to get into it. They sat waiting for a few minutes. Then Tertio, who had opened up considerably under the influence of the evening's wine, said he was going to take the crocodile for a short walk on its elastic lead, to test its shuffles and gyrations in action.

Tania stayed where she was, staring out at the road ahead, dappled by shadows, but now and again brilliantly lit by the spasmodic flare of an exploding firework.

It was one such glow of light, prolonged by another immediately after it which caught Vicente and Sophia in tableau, as it were. They were some twenty-five yards from the car, standing in a close embrace, Sophia's body arched to the pressure of his, her head flung back in abandonment to the long kiss they exchanged while Tania watched in shocked incredulous dismay at an intimacy which must have made such a kiss possible.

Vicente and Sophia—*lovers*? Of a night only? Of a week? Of how long? And if for longer than tonight's coming together, how blind had she

been in supposing Sophia's aim had been acceptance into the Massimo circle, when her real
quarry must have been Vicente himself . . . Benno
lost to her, she had decided to look higher for a
protector, and if, on tonight's seeming, she had
succeeded, what did that make of their front of
mere acquaintanceship for public consumption?
For Tania's and Fabia's deception? A cruel sham.

It was dark again. Tertio came back, reporting
that the crocodile had wriggled satisfactorily to
order, and the other two, indifferently apart now,
arrived at opposite doors of the car. The evening's
sights and experiences were exchanged (how dis-
creetly edited? Tania wondered), and they turned
for home.

They gathered in the *salotto* for a last drink.
The Rienzis had left and Fabia had gone to bed.
Tertio rode noisily away and Vicente saw Sophia
out to her car. As Fabia's deputy hostess, Tania
felt she should suggest that Vicente should see
her back to her apartment. But Sophia, sure of
her evening's conquest, if of no more, could afford
to decline. She had, she said, 'a little man' of long-
standing service who was to meet her in his *moto'
scafo* at the Roma quay, and would walk her home
from Accademia for a few extra lire. She *must* not
usurp Vicente's company for a moment longer of
a most *enchanting* evening, she declared, and
underlined the falsity of that with a judas kiss for
Tania's cheek. She had learned her lesson of discretion from long practice in her affair with
Benno, Tania decided. Now she was putting it to

use in hoodwinking Vicente's wife.

Tania heard her car drive away, and was play-ing idly with the crocodile when Vicente came back. She stood up and simulated a yawn, though in fact she was too tense for sleep. Vicente said, 'Tired? A pity. I'd thought we might make a night of it.'

She stared at him, her heart pounding. 'A——? I thought we'd made one?'

'A duty foursome only.' (*Duty?*) 'I'd been thinking along the lines of the cruise on the lagoon which we haven't taken yet. What do you say?'

Straight from Sophia's arms to offer a sop to her! Tania knew she ought to have the moral indignation to refuse it, and scorning to play the shrew by accusing him, leave him to guess why. But somehow she could not. Later her pride would pay with shame. But better a crust than no bread . . . She cleared her throat nervously. 'It's very late,' she said.

'All the better for getting the water to ourselves. Even the gondoliers will be in bed. Can you go as you are?' He helped her into the short-sleeved coat she had thrown over a chair, and waited while she tied a headscarf.

On the drive to Roma to pick up his launch she wondered what had prompted him to suggest this excursion, and could only suppose he was guiltily conscious that he had neglected her for Sophia during the evening. But though that might be the reaction of some men, self-blame was so alien to Vicente's arrogance that she doubted it. She longed for a rapport between them which could question him easily and naturally as to why he wanted to prolong the evening until near dawn—with her, for whose companionship he seemed to have little need.

They boarded the launch at the della Croce quay and slid out into the scarcely ruffled water of the Grand Canal. On either side the ancient, legendary buildings were fretted silhouettes against the dark sky, the campanile of San Marco a heaven-pointing finger, the under-shadows of the bridges caverns of blackness. As they sped downstream Vicente pointed out landmarks as if, Tania thought wryly, he were conducting her on a guided tour. Though why choose the middle of the night for it, if that were all it was?

They were past the south-eastern point of the mainland now, and out on the open lagoon. The fashionable Lido lay to the south, but Vicente turned in among the archipelagos of tiny islands, too small to be named, mere dark masses ahead and astern. Tania wondered how often he had travelled these waterways with superb navigation, but remembering his assured claim that Venice was 'his' city, she supposed he included all its unique environs in that. And he confirmed this when a little later he switched off and allowed the launch to drift and circle idly as it would. He operated the switch which turned their seats into recliners, and laid an arm carelessly across the back of Tania's.

He said, 'Some time ago you were trying to pin

down the romance of Venice, and you seemed to think me smug for saying I hadn't to look for it; I possessed it, as all Venetians do, as their birthright. And this—' his spread hand indicated the silent, tideless expanse around them—'the water that is the whole how and why of the city's being as it is, we've made our servant too.' He paused. 'When, that is, it isn't our master. But over the centuries we've learned to live with that.'

He had never spoken with such intensity before—as if he wanted her to understand and even share his feeling for the city, which, however incredible, she found disarming.

She said, 'I didn't think you smug. I—envied you.'

'Being without a clue yourself to any such sense of committed possession?'

'Wishing I had a clue, rather,' she admitted. 'But I've never known anything quite like Venice to be beholden *to*.' She added shyly, 'To—to love so deeply that I felt it was mine.'

'Nor any*one*? No man? Before or since Benno, since obviously you didn't love him?'

'I did once.'

'Thought you did, and found it asked too much of you,' he contradicted. 'But you haven't answered my question—before or since him?'

Though she wanted to deny him the right to ask, she said, 'Before Benno, there was no one. And since—I've been your wife, haven't I?'

'Not all the time since,' he corrected dryly. 'There was a certain hiatus when——'

At that her patience broke. 'You mean when I was seeing Pascale Fedore?' she flared. 'Well, you can believe this now or never, for I won't *stoop* to telling you again! Pascale meant nothing to me— nothing but as a friend of Benno's whom I liked too. You may have thought you had to marry me to break it up between us, but you were utterly wrong! There was no need to cheat us out of meeting again, nor of forbidding me to see him when he came back from abroad.'

Vicente gave a short laugh. 'My dear girl, I married you for quite other reasons than to prise you away from the young man, whom I could have seen off in half a dozen lesser ways.' He leaned away from her in his seat and scrutinised her. 'Do you really suppose I needed to use the sledgehammer of marriage to crack the nut of your flirtation with Fedore?'

'You allowed me to think so,' she murmured.

'Pff! It simply tied in with my real motives for the marriage.'

She nodded. 'To see that I atoned for Benno, and to comfort Madrigna with grandchildren. None of the things that marriage ought to be about.'

'Such things being?'

'You must know.' She looked at him helplessly. 'Love, respect, companionship. The—the other person being the only one in the world one wants to live with—and for. The *only* one.'

He answered with flat logic, 'You married me for reasons of your own, you said. I didn't bear you, screaming, to the altar. That being so, can you claim that your motives were any less self-interested or more romantic than mine appeared?'

Tania remembered her revenge and shook her head. 'No.'

'Then has either of us any more right than the other to feel cheated of romance?'

'I—suppose not.' It took courage to add, 'But you—— You cheat me of everything else, other than your name and your roof and—and your bed. I don't *know* you.' Her voice rose in panic protest. 'I don't know anything about you! For you, I might not be here, or anywhere where you are, or anywhere at all, unless or until you choose to have me there. For what?' She spread her hands emptily. 'I've never known!'

'Sometimes you must have known. And why,' he put in quietly, in contrast with her railing tone.

Tania flushed. 'For *that*—yes.' But only for that.

Vicente was silent, as if she had indeed given him food for thought. Then he echoed, ' "That"? Which you don't rate as important in your ideal of marriage?'

He was confusing her. 'Of course I do,' she protested. 'It—it *is* marriage.'

'Exactly. So that, if I had gone through the ceremony and left you as virgin as you were before it, shouldn't I have cheated you of even more? Not to mention forgoing rights of my own which I had warned you I meant to exact?'

'In marrying me without love,' she finished for him.

'In marrying you on equal terms which neither of us disclosed,' he corrected. 'Marrying you on a mutual agreement which so far you have honoured, in that I've never had to rape you in order to get my way with you.' As if on a second thought he added, 'Honoured, that is, if I can believe you about Fedore.'

'You can,' she assured him.

'I'm glad.'

That touched her as the most simple admission she had ever heard him make. Her heart lightened. They had talked and Vicente had listened and seemed to care that she accepted where they both stood. He hadn't ignored her nor dismissed her; he had *invited* her to share with him an aspect of the city he loved. That must mean some hope for a future they couldn't escape? This was a first time of reaching for each other. There would be others. There had to be . . .! In the heady optimism of her mood she could afford to forget that, only an hour or two earlier, she had seen him kiss Sophia Greniere with passion. She might remember and doubt him again. But not tonight. Not tonight.

Vicente pressed her shoulders lightly and withdrew his arm from the back of her seat. He flicked his own to the upright and switched on his engine. 'Time we went home,' he said, and whether or not he intended it, she read promise into that; promise that this night of new accord with him hadn't yet done its best with her.

Nor had it. For once Vicente hadn't left her but had stayed to sleep in their marriage bed, while beside him she lay sleepless but fulfilled, reluctant to let the night slip away into a memory and a misty Venetian dawn.

He had led her to enjoy their love-play as gently as on that first night of marriage which she had so dreaded. Then, afterwards, she had despised her body for betraying her into pleasure at his hands. But this time it had all seemed so right—the ache of her longing for him as inevitable as a sea's high tide drawing to its breaking on a shore. In the growing desire to which he had roused her she had heard herself plead, 'Love me ... care about me,' and his response had spoken in the surge of passion which took them, panting and all-giving, to their culmination.

There was peace now, the slow downturn from rapture, this time not to despair and self-loathing, but to near-confidence.

From now on it was all going to be easier. After this it couldn't *not* be easier to reach Vicente in talk, questions asked and answered without reserve; even plans laid together and carried out.

That was one thought which Tania took with her into sleep at last. The other was a prayer to her fate. If she were to bear a child to Vicente, let it have been conceived in the ecstasy just past ...

CHAPTER EIGHT

IT was easier. There was a day when Vicente invited her to hostess a party of foreign buyers, first on a tour of the Crystos island foundry and then for lunch at the city showrooms, when, unlike that first business dinner party, he seemed at pains to emphasise her role as something more than a decorative background figure. By leaving the conducting of individual buyers to her, he seemed to acknowledge for the first time that she knew enough about the glass industry to be informative on it. In an informal after-lunch speech he even told his hearers that Crystos was fortunate in his choice of a wife!

When a world-famous prima donna visited the Teatro Fenice for a single performance of *Traviata*, he made up a small party (which did not include Sophia), dining first at the Gritti Palace and going on afterwards to Florian's for supper. He invited Tania to fly with him to Rome when he had a day's business there and where he left her to window-shop on Veneto and Condotti, telling her to buy something for herself which she thought he would approve, charging it to him if she shopped at Luigi's on Condotti, where he had an account. Meeting him afterwards, when she confessed to having charged a fabulous sum for a shirt of thick cream Italian silk, he insisted that she add a matching jacket. On the way back to the airport he said, 'We must do historic and religious Rome another time'—making it sound like a promise he would keep.

Occasionally he would come home early from the city and invite Tania to swim. Neither Sophia's name nor Pascale's was mentioned between them during those days. Tania almost forgot about the mission she had left with Pascale, and told herself that she must and could— almost—believe that Vicente's affair with Sophia had begun and ended on that night of *festa* at Padua.

Then the illusion that he had begun to forgive her and that they were growing closer was suddenly shattered. There was an evening when Vicente arrived late for dinner, kissed Fabia and apologised to her, did not address Tania directly throughout the meal and left the table before coffee was served. On his way out of the room, 'I'd like to see you when you have finished, please. I shall be in my study if you will come there,' he told Tania in a tone so coldly formal that it did not escape Fabia, who commented wryly over the coffee-cups, 'That is his "juvenile delinquent" voice which used to irritate poor Benno so much. But he really shouldn't use it to you. How do you suppose you have annoyed him, if you have?'

Tania said, 'I don't know. I don't feel very guilty.' She defended Vicente, 'He probably didn't realise he sounded as curt as he did.' But when he had been keeping her at the arm's length of his contempt she had heard that glacial note too often before, not to fear its threat now. She finished her coffee at a gulp. 'Better go and see which garden gate I left open,' she grimaced re-assuringly at Fabia, and went.

Vicente attacked as soon as she had closed the study door behind her. He had been sitting at his desk but he stood now and did not invite her to sit. 'Why were you so concerned to make me believe Pascale Fedore meant nothing to you, when it wasn't true?' he demanded.

Tania caught her breath, but felt on safe ground. 'It was true, and is,' she said.

'True too, you'd claim, that you haven't seen him by appointment since I forbade your meeting him and prevented your doing so?' he flung at her.

That was more difficult. But 'by appointment' let her conscience out, and with her own secrets to keep, Sophia wasn't likely to have broken her cynical pact to tell no one about the loan of her apartment to Pascale for their meeting. Feeling still on firm ground, Tania echoed, 'True too—I haven't made any appointment to see him.'

'Which is a lie.'

'It's the truth!'

The dark fire of anger in his eyes should have warned her. Very deliberately he asked, 'Then how do you explain your having spent long hours of rendezvous with the man in Sophia Greniere's apartment, which he had begged of her for the purpose?'

Tania realised that her involuntary gasp of dismay had betrayed her to him. She could only stammer, 'I—I didn't——'

'Oh, come!' he scorned.

'—didn't arrange to meet him. Didn't know he was going to be there. And I didn't stay for "hours".'

'From early evening to a little this side of midnight, I understood?'

'*No!*'

'Can you prove that?'

She remembered Sophia's taunt that she wouldn't stoop to reliance on servants' evidence, and she didn't mean to. If Vicente couldn't believe her without proof——! 'No,' she said. 'Both you and Madrigna were out that night until after I came back. In fact, I don't know when either of you came in. I'd gone to bed.'

'Then you admit there was such a meeting; you remember the evening well, but were prepared to lie about it?'

'*Not* to lie. Not to deny that Pascale was alone in Sophia's apartment when I went there. But certainly to deny I was expecting to see him.' Slightly emboldened, Tania added, 'May I ask how you knew I had seen him after you told me I shouldn't? Have you had me *followed*?'

'When I had given you credit for understanding that an affair with him wouldn't do? Of course not. No, I had the truth from Sophia herself when she lunched with me today.'

'You lunched with her? I didn't know you

were seeing her!'

'Or you would have been afraid of what she could tell me?'

Tania snapped, 'She didn't tell you the truth. And I suppose you can take her out to lunch, but I mustn't see a friend of *mine* without asking your permission?'

'If your story is true that you were surprised to see Fedore you can hardly have consulted me beforehand,' Vicente retorted unanswerably. 'And a lunch date in a public restaurant isn't exactly a parallel with a contrived secret meeting at night in an empty apartment. For you don't dispute, I hope, that Fedore arranged it with Sophia, telling her he "had" to see you?'

'It wasn't arranged with me!'

'Though you took advantage of the chance to spend the evening alone with him. You stayed, did you not?'

'For a little while, yes.'

'Long enough, I daresay, for the staging of a touching reunion, or for as long as you thought it safe. Sophia had left drinks for you which were used, and she concluded, from Fedore's enthusiastic thanks and flowers, that the tête-à-tête had enjoyed an enormous success.'

'Admitting she connived at it, but still thought it her duty to report it to you?' Tania demanded bitterly.

'It wouldn't have been news to me if, with allegedly nothing to hide, you had seen fit to report it yourself,' Vicente pointed out.

'And since I didn't——?'

'Since you didn't, the conclusions are obvious—that, whether or not you began as an innocent party, you didn't remain one, and didn't want me to know.'

His injustice infuriated her. She might argue for hours but would not convince him. She counter-attacked instead.

'Any more, I expect,' she took him up, 'than you've wanted me to know when you've been seeing Sophia Greniere without telling me. Lunch today—for the first time, you would have me believe?'

'By no means.' His smooth tone contrasted with the tartness of hers as her sense of injury ran away with her control.

Her voice rasping, she scorned, 'I thought not. And lunch indeed! Tell me, what's so innocent about midday, when there's the whole afternoon to follow? Don't tell *me* it's only Frenchmen who entertain their mistresses in the afternoon before they go home to their wives in the evening! You were even late for dinner——'

She got no further. One stride brought Vicente close enough to clamp her by the wrist and to administer a smart slap to her cheek.

'Oh——!' Her fingers went to guard it and tears of shock blurred her eyes. The smack hadn't been a brutal one nor very painful. Its sting was in its surprise and in its conclusive check to her tirade. She must have sounded like an abusive shrew or a raving hysteric, only to be silenced by such treatment, and it had underlined his contempt of her as little else could. She saw the brittle accord they had achieved disappear in their new distrust, and could have wept for the promise it had had, and had no longer.

Vicente released her wrist and waited. 'That's better,' he told her lowered eyes and set mouth. And then, 'When I am caught *in flagrante delicto* with Sophia Greniere, that will be time enough for your fishwife accusations of guilt. Not before.'

'But you can judge me for the same kind of guilt without any proof at all!' she protested mutinously, though vainly, she knew.

'Ah, but there's nothing clandestine about my entertaining Sophia and I don't find it necessary to lie to achieve it. There is a difference,' he said.

He had closed his mind against her, she thought. If only she could close herself, mind and body, from him!

She had left Fabia with a wry joke about his summons to her, and hadn't prepared any explanation of it when she returned to the *salotto*. But as if she sensed trouble which would not be confided to her, Fabia asked no questions and made no comment when Vicente did not join them. She and Tania watched television and chatted until they agreed it was time to go to bed.

In her room Tania remembered another time when, arrogant and possessive even in his anger, Vicente had demanded his male right to her body, utterly uncaring that every fibre in her was recoiling from him, as from rape.

That mustn't happen again tonight. She couldn't bear it. She locked her door. And did so the next night, and the next. Vicente did not try the handle, nor remark on her withdrawal. And when she left it unlocked again, he did not come. They were again the strangers they had been on their wedding day.

For all Vicente's disclaimer of a guilty intimacy with Sophia, she would not have broken the pact of silence she had forced on Tania if she had not felt sure of her influence with him, Tania felt. Whatever she hoped to gain by the affair, she must feel sure enough of her ground as his potential mistress—if she wasn't that already—to have lost her fear of anything Tania could tell him of her association with Benno. One brother as vulnerable to her charm as another—what cause could the present one find for blaming her guilty past with the other? Tania decided she would argue so and feel safe. Let Tania do her worst with the story! She could live it down.

And she *was* safe while Tania was tied to silence by her own scruples and her need to uncover for herself the truth about Benno's intrigues. And her fervour to achieve that heightened during these bleak days of the realisation that Vicente seemed to be signalling to her that he had finished with her as a trusted wife.

Her rebellion grew. If he could claim innocence because he made no secret of meeting Sophia, then she would see Pascale as openly if or when he had any news for her. She would tell Fabia when she would be out and with whom, and leave Fabia to vouch to Vicente that there was nothing clandestine about it. And whatever Vicente's reaction, the rift between them could scarcely grow wider than it was now.

She waited for a sign from Pascale through several weeks of a Venetian late summer of heat which dissolved, intermittently at first, and then finally, into autumnal rains and gales in which the river Brenta levelled with its banks, the surrounding marshes became swamps and the low-lying squares of the city resembled shallow lakes. This was normal for the time of year, Tania learned. Venice in winter was at the mercy of its surrounding water, but only in exceptional years did it face panic conditions and danger to life. Meanwhile the summer tourists went home and the city settled down to its business and social winter of trade exhibitions and film festivals and the opera season with its consequent parties.

It was on one such day of storm that there was a letter from Pascale in Tania's mail. It asked simply that she should see him. If she could reach Piazzale Roma by eleven, he would meet her. No need to let him know; he would be there and would wait for her.

Tania went with the letter to Fabia. 'May I have Rietti and the car?' she asked.

'Why, of course, *cara*.' Fabia looked out at the lashing rain. 'But what a day to choose! You may not be able to get down the Canal.'

'It won't matter. I'm only meeting Pascale Fedore for a talk, and we needn't leave Roma; we could go to a café or even stay in the car.' (Hardly, with Rietti in the driver's seat, was Tania's mental reservation.) But Fabia, reassured, agreed,

'Of course. Or if you preferred to go to a restaurant, you could send Rietti back and ring Vicente to ask him to bring you home, and perhaps your friend Pascale too, to lunch?'

'No, I think perhaps I will keep Rietti,' said Tania, knowing she would.

Pascale was pacing the car park beside his own car when she arrived. She asked Rietti to wait for her and joined him. The nearby cafés were full and noisy, but they found a comparatively quiet corner where they could talk.

'You have heard something which could help me?' she asked.

'It's possible,' Pascale nodded. 'No more than hearsay, but it could have a bearing. You'll know about the International Crystal Fair next month? Well, there's a story going about that the Crystos stand will be showing something unique and secret and only just developed, and it struck me——'

Tania caught her breath. 'You think it could be what I fear—that Benno did find something in my father's papers, and Crystos have made use of it?'

'It's impossible to say, without knowing what form the development takes. If it were anything on the heavy side of the industry, like the mix or the firing or the blowing, I'd say it couldn't have been perfected in the time. If it were anything lighter—the engraving, the cutting—yes, perhaps. It's a pity you have no idea what line your father's ideas may have followed,' Pascale deplored.

'And I haven't, though I should doubt they were about the big fundamentals. Our foundry was only in a very small way. It's much more likely he had hit on something to do with the finish of the glass,' said Tania.

'Whatever it was, Benno seemed to think it would make you rich. But short of smuggling an industrial spy into Crystos, we are going to have to wait until the Fair to find out what they are keeping under wraps.'

'Yes.' Tania was facing an outcome in which, ever since she had realised she loved Vicente, she hadn't wanted to believe. But if the novelty had had its origin in her father's brain, then its purloining by Benno must have been furthered by Vicente, master-minding the project to a success which Benno hadn't lived to achieve. That meant that, along with Benno's effects, her father's papers *had* passed to Vicente, who had claimed they did not exist—

She roused from her musing to hear Pascale putting the same thought into words as tactfully as he could. 'With the thing having its debut at the Fair, I'm afraid it has to be your husband's development,' he said. 'Is that going to make any difference to your wanting the fraud—if there's been one—exposed?'

Tania hesitated. Then, 'No,' she said. 'If it was a theft by Benno, and Vicente has made use of it—no.'

Pascale looked at her pityingly. 'You have a desperate courage,' he said. 'But I wonder if you realise how hard it could be for you if you make your husband your enemy?'

She longed to reply, 'He has already made himself my enemy.' But she did not. She knew Pascale was asking, as he had done before, though in different words, what would happen to her marriage if she could prove Vicente guilty, and she must not give him the hope that it would be over. For it would not. To all outward seeming at least, Vicente would see to that.

She told Pascale that Sophia had tried to make trouble over their meeting at the apartment, but not how far she had succeeded, nor that Sophia and Vicente had become unlikely intimates. She also told him she had made no secret of their date this morning. To which he said eagerly, 'Then perhaps we can do it again some time—in better weather?' And, 'Yes, perhaps,' she replied, smiling, though despising her need to make use of him for ends which she now dreaded to face.

But she had set her hand to the plough . . .

Buoyed by her new spirit of rebellion, Tania decided to leave her meeting with Pascale to Fabia's casual mention to Vicente, and felt she was justified when, in answer to Fabia's chatty remark, 'Tania was in the city this morning, seeing Benno's friend Pascale Fedore,' he merely said, 'Really?' and looking across the dinner table at Tania, 'You must have had a stormy trip?'

'Yes, but we only met for coffee on Roma. I was home for lunch,' she said. Which Vicente acknowledged with a cool nod and no more questions, confirming, as she had suspected, that her movements were no longer of interest to him. Or if they were, and he was still secretly watchful of her, he was not letting her guess it, probably deeming that his very indifference would bring her to heel.

Her heart sank. Too often she had heard from married couples, 'We go our own ways', and though she and Vicente had gone only so very briefly together, it seemed they might now be essentially apart for good.

She realised that something of the tension between them must have got through to her mother-in-law when, a few days later, Fabia questioned, 'Do you know whether Vicente has any reason to dislike Signor Fedore? I ask because, though I know he took you out several times before he went abroad and you married, we've never invited him here, and we should.'

Tania said, 'I think Vicente felt I saw too much of him too soon after Benno's death.'

Fabia nodded. 'That could be so. He is so watchful of any possible scandal for us. But there was nothing wrong in your friendship, was there?'

'None at all,' Tania assured her, knowing she could deny the kind of 'wrong' which was meant.

'And naturally the young man wanted to see you again when he came back to Venice, as I shall tell Vicente, and that we ought to offer him some hospitality, if only for Benno's sake, though perhaps not before the Fair, which is taking everyone's attention just now. I expect Vicente will have told you about the big Gala dinner for the foreign buyers on the eve of the Fair?' Fabia added, changing the subject, to Tania's relief.

With the Fair no more than a fortnight away, it was an event for which the whole of the Venetian glass industry had 'before' and 'after' plans. This piece of business must be handled before it; that could safely be left until after. It was an attitude which filtered through to the social scene, with the Gala and the Fair high points of agreeable entertainment beyond which engagement diaries need not look. But for Tania they were a kind of watershed between her present nagging doubts and speculations and the possible ugly certainties to be faced afterwards. The nervous strain of alternate hope and dread robbed her of both sleep and appetite, and one evening, going to join Fabia and Vicente at dinner, from the doorway the room seemed to spin before her eyes, and she slid down the doorpost in a faint.

Instantly Vicente was there, gathering her up, pressing her head down into the hollow of his shoulder and supporting her with an arm about her as her moment of unconsciousness passed.

Fabia hovered behind him, clucking compassion and concern. Then she was carried to the windowseat and laid upon it, and Vicente stood looking down at her, his fingers on the pulse at her wrist. 'What was the cause of that?' he asked.

Her eyes were properly in focus now. 'I don't know. It's nothing. I'm quite all right,' she said, and sat up to prove it.

He pressed her down again and Fabia slipped a cushion under her head.. 'A faint is never "nothing",' he said. 'I'll bring Dr Carloni out to you.'

'Oh no, please. If I'm not better tomorrow— But I shall be. I am already.'

'Can you take any dinner? Just a little bowl of *brodo ristretto*, perhaps?' Fabia urged.

Tania hid a shudder of distaste for even clear soup. 'Just a glass of *aqua seltz* and a dry biscuit. And perhaps—I'll go to bed.'

'Of course. I will come with you. The best thing you can do,' Fabia approved, and Vicente let them go without further mention of the doctor.

Tania sipped her soda water by the light of her bedside lamp. She could always sleep at the beginning of the night—the hours of wakefulness began nearer to morning—and some time later she started out of a doze to find the lamp still on and that someone was standing at the half-open door.

'Madrigna?' she questioned. 'I've been asleep already——' But it was Vicente, not Fabia, who came across to her bedside.

'Did I wake you?' he asked.

'I don't think so. It was the light on my eyes, I think.' She put up a hand to push aside a strand of hair, but his was there first, thrusting back her hair before it touched her temple and then her brow.

'Quite cool. You are really better?' he asked.

'Yes, I told you——'

'Do you want anything?'

(Yes, yes, her anguish clamoured. To hold out my arms to you, to find myself in yours, and to cry and cry on your shoulder, begging you to forgive me for doubting you, whatever you are, whatever wrong you may have done me——) Aloud she said, 'No, thank you. I expect I shall sleep again quite quickly.'

He nodded, made a business of smoothing sheet and coverlet and with a finger on the lamp-switch looked his question as to whether he should put out the light.

'Yes, please.' So that it was to the sudden darkness between them that she heard him say, 'Is there anything you want to tell me?'

Her heart lurched with fear of the menace she read into the ordinary words. What *could* he think she was holding back from him, unless by some means he had learned of her intrigue against him and Benno? It was impossible. No one knew of it but loyal Pascale, and she could trust him. Yes, for all the weight the question had had for her guilt, Vicente must be referring to something else, something quite trivial. The thought buoyed her to answer lightly, 'To tell you? Something I've forgotten? No, I don't think so. What?'

There was a moment of fraught silence. Then Vicente said, 'It does not matter. My mistake.' She heard him go out and the door closing behind him.

His mistake! If he had left it at 'It doesn't matter' she could have believed it didn't, and could have calmed down. But his claim that he had expected something from her and was disappointed altered everything. The insomnia lying in wait for her was stark with imaginings and regrets.

She got up wearily, wondering if she could use her last night's malaise to suggest she have a few days to herself in, say, Rome or Florence. But she had been too ready to protest there was nothing wrong with her to justify that. And besides, Pascale might have more news for her which she must not miss. But apparently he had not, for by the eve of the Fair he had made no sign.

The half-dozen luxury hotels of the city took it in yearly turn to be the venue of the Dinner, as did the major crystal firms to house the Fair in their city showrooms. For the nights of the Dinner and the Fair the Villa was to be host to two Germans, buying for their stores in Dusseldorf and Berlin; both formally correct gentlemen, speaking excellent Italian. They arrived on the morning of the Dinner, and in Vicente's absence on last-minute arrangements, Fabia and Tania entertained them at lunch.

The talk, naturally, was mainly of glass. At one

point Herr Hoffe remarked, 'Of course we come
to Venice, and are not disappointed, for our top
market requirements. But for our middle-line
sales we find we have to look to Czechoslovakia
or Austria. They understand the needs of the mass
market better than anyone else.'

Fabia suggested, 'I have heard my stepson say
that their labour costs are much lower than ours,'
while Tania supplemented, 'And for mass pro-
duction they can't command and probably don't
need the master craftsmen who are at a premium
here.'

'That is assuredly so,' Herr Hoffe agreed. 'All
the same, there seems no reason why some enter-
prising foundry in Venice shouldn't consider ex-
ploiting the lower-bracket market alongside the
quality one.'

'We may find at the Fair that someone has anticipated the idea,' Herr Seigmann offered.

'Perhaps. It's said that we can expect some
novelties.' Herr Hoffe turned with a smile to
Tania. 'For instance, *signora*, there are some interesting rumours coming from Crystos. But I suppose I must not expect you to confirm the truth
of those before the Fair opens?'

Tania's answering smile was thin. 'I couldn't,
even if I were willing, *mein Herr*. For I don't
know the truth of them myself.'

'No? Then we must be patient and wait. And
believe me, I have no wish to probe your confidence, *signora*. It was simply that the word has
gone about that, whatever the innovation Signor

Massimo has to spring on us, it was English-inspired, and knowing you yourself are English-born and versed in crystal, one wondered——'
Herr Hoffe's apologia trailed into silence and Tania's taut-drawn breath and jerked head were tactfully covered by Fabia's gentle,

'You understand, *mein Herr*, Vicente is a true Massimo, in that for him, as for my late husband, their home is their home and their craft their craft, and neither is allowed to trouble the other unduly. Therefore, though we may hear rumours——'

'In other words,' put in Herr Seigmann, now trying out his English, ' "Never the twain shall meet." As the English say, do they not?'

Trying out his own, 'A Scottish saying, I *think*, Herman,' Herr Hoffe rebuked his friend.

'Rudyard Kipling, in fact,' Tania corrected, her tone mechanical, absent, while *English-inspired*, *English-inspired* echoed and hammered in her brain. After that, dared she hope that Vicente wasn't guilty?

She and Fabia had shopped together for their dinner dresses. Fabia would still consider nothing but black for herself, but she had persuaded Tania to silver brocade, slim and sheathlike to her knees where fan-pleated gussets fluted in and out as she walked; the most sophisticated gown she had ever possessed, but she was enchanted with it, and was disposed to be rebellious when Fabia had made her parade it for Vicente's approval.

'Do you mean that if he doesn't like it, I must wear something else?' she had asked. To which

Fabia had replied,

'I think there is no fear he will not like it. But the Dinner, you understand, is one of the biggest occasions of his year, and for this, his first as a married man, I know you will want him to be proud of showing off his wife.'

It had been on the tip of Tania's bitter tongue to retort, 'Showing off how he can afford to dress his wife, don't you mean?' But of course she had not said it, and on one of the very few evenings now that Vicente was at home, she had put on the dress and called him into her room to see it.

He had looked her up and down with a connoisseur's eye. 'For the Dinner?' he had asked.

'Yes. Will it do?'

'Whoever is your dinner partner should be the envy of the rest of us,' he said—cool, impersonal praise with which she had to be content, though she would have given anything for him to have said something like, 'What's so important about a dress? *You* would look lovely in a bathrobe'—and to have meant it.

Their party broke up as soon as they arrived at the hotel. Tania left Fabia with some friends and went in search of Pascale in the crowded foyer and lounge-bars. It was he who saw her first and disengaged himself from a group of his Vetro Mestiere colleagues. She felt his touch upon her arm and turned. 'Oh, Pascale——!'

She saw his admiring look, but could take no pleasure in it. 'It's true!' she panted. 'I've heard more since I saw you. Have you? That, whatever it is that Crystos are introducing, the idea for the process came from England? Which means——'

'Yes, I've heard that too. But only today,' said Pascale.

They stood looking at each other in silence, sharing the same doubts.

CHAPTER NINE

VICENTE came into her room the next morning at the same time as Tania's early coffee was brought. 'I'm going in to the Fair now,' he said. 'You need not come until it opens, but people will want to see and be introduced to you on the Crystos stand, so I hope you can give most of the day to being there?'

'I'd meant to,' she told him.

'Good. Rietti can take you and Madrigna to Roma; the Herrs are making their own arrangements, but I'll send the launch back to pick you two up there.'

'Yes, do that.' As he nodded and turned to go she added, 'You know, last night everyone was talking about the Crystos surprise packet, as somebody called it. So if I'm to be on the stand and you are showing it, oughtn't I to know what it is? For there is one, isn't there, though you haven't told even Madrigna anything about it?'

He turned back. 'We've developed a new process, yes. The process our industrial secret, of course. But we're showing the first results on the stand.'

'What are they?'

'You will see them for yourself. You'd better come along before the Opening, and I will show them to you.'

'You are mysterious!' She tried to speak lightly before putting the question which really mattered. 'Has the process, whatever it is, taken a long time to develop?'

'Long enough. And we turned the last key to the solution, as it were, only quite recently.'

She moistened lips gone suddenly dry. 'Really? S-since when?'

'Only this summer.'

Tania waited. This was the point at which, if he meant to confess that the successfully turned 'key' had been her father's contribution to the affair, he would have to say so. If he said nothing more in explanation, that made him guilty—didn't it?

He said nothing more. With an urgent glance at his watch he was on his way again, and she let him go. He had made his one mistake by admitting that the project had been perfected only since she had come to Venice, with her father's papers in Benno's care, and since then passed to Vicente. That, she felt, was enough proof to take to Pascale. But after that—what?

When she went downstairs she found that Rietti had orders to drive her and Fabia early enough for them to arrive an hour before the Fair's official opening by a member of the Government.

'A kind of private view for us,' commented Fabia. 'I told Vicente before he left this morning very early, that he owed us that.' That, and a lot more than that to me, was Tania's bitter thought as they set out.

The show hall was a brilliant contrast to the dark day outside. Glass glittered and sparkled, its facets taking every colour in the spectrum from the light of magnificent chandeliers. The best of the Venetian traditional craft was there for the interest of the world. Salesmen were everywhere, gossiping in groups, putting last touches to their own stands, quizzing those of their competitors.

Tania's first interest was to locate the Crystos stand, her second to look for Pascale. But she had not seen him when Vicente came to make a way for Fabia and herself through the crowd around his stand.

It was not difficult to see that the attraction was a background triptych inscribed in gold lettering 'Cristallo Fiore', against which were displayed vases, decanters and wine goblets, from the liqueur shape to the champagne tulip, all hand-painted in delicate designs, from flower clusters to a contrast of pastoral scenes and severe futuristic patterns.

From the gasps and muttered comments of the audience, it was obvious that the achievement was unique. In Tania's experience there was nothing like it on the market, and Fabia caught at Vicente's sleeve.

'Hand-painting *after* firing and shaping? How, Vicente, how?' she urged.

His glance travelled over the crowd about the stand. 'Wouldn't all these gentlemen like to know?' he retorted—a sally which was greeted with guffaws of disbelief that they would be told.

He drew Tania and Fabia aside, and Fabia went on, 'Your father worked on it for years, I know; it was one of the few problems he apologised for "troubling" me with. But you!—you have succeeded!' She turned to Tania. 'Your husband is a genius on crystal, *cara*!' And back to Vicente, 'How long has it taken you?' Tania had never seen her so animated, and was glad to be spared making any comment of her own. She recognised that Crystos had accomplished a process hitherto regarded as wishful thinking, but Pascale would have to tell her how well grounded was her suspicion that Benno had lighted upon and purloined the secret, and Vicente had used it.

He was answering Fabia, 'Two years and more. We've had designers at work all over the country; our own artists painting on as fine a weight of crystal as is acceptable in a drinking vessel—only for the whole thing to fuse in the firing to set the colours and the design, leaving us, time and again, with a heap of ashes.'

'But you did succeed?'

'Only by mere chance. As with all the best inventions, there was a missing link which eluded us until only this summer.' He turned back to the stand and handed them each an item to examine. 'Not a noticeably commercial proposition. But there is always a market for the best, and Crystos isn't interested in anything less,' he commented.

'They will be collectors' pieces and heirlooms,' Fabia claimed.

'One hopes so.' There was a new stir now; the

Fair was about to be opened, and Vicente, due on the platform, excused himself and left them. He seemed not to have noticed Tania's silence.

Afterwards Fabia remained behind the Crystos stand and Tania went in search of Pascale, busy with Vetro Mestiere clients, but willing to give her the hearing she begged of him.

'Have you seen it?' she asked, guessing he would have done.

He nodded. 'And you too, of course?'

'Yes.'

'And are happier? As relieved as I hope you are and should be?'

She frowned. 'Relieved? You think I can be? Why?'

'Why?' he echoed. 'Because, dear girl, knowing what you do of crystal processing, you must know that this crucible firing of the finished article must have taken years to perfect?'

'More than two, Vicente says,' she agreed.

'And therefore—*therefore*—work it out for yourself.'

'You mean,' she hesitated, 'that the experiments on these prototypes must have taken too long? Too long, that is, for the idea to have been stolen by Benno from my father?'

'Exactly that. By any standards there simply has not been time.'

'Even though Vicente admits that they had failure after failure until a final missing piece fell into place *only this summer*?' Tania countered darkly.

Pascale looked taken aback. 'He said that? What was it?'

'He didn't enlarge. He never talks technicalities to his stepmother or me. But that makes possible Benno's theft of at least that last link, don't you see? And what did Benno mean by telling you I was sitting on an unsuspected goldmine, if there hadn't been anything *to* steal, or to marry me in order to get?'

At that Pascale's glance was pitying. 'My dear, isn't it time, for your own happiness, that you forgot that eavesdropping of yours?' he urged. 'Benno is dead. You are married to Vicente—of your own decision, you say, and you mean to stand by your marriage, whatever the outcome of all this. So what do you gain by raking through the chances that they have both cheated you? You only destroy yourself instead of them.'

'I have a right to the truth about Benno,' Tania maintained.

'*And* about Vicente?'

'He must have used the idea that Benno stole. He has been over to England since we were married. And even our two German guests at the Villa had heard that it came from England.'

'So what are you going to do about it?'

'I—don't know. I think I was hoping you might tell me.'

Pascale shook his head. 'On as little proof as you have, I couldn't advise you to accuse him. Even if you put a spy into Crystos to locate the formula, it would be the word of Crystos against yours that it originated with your father.'

'And I haven't any "word"! I don't know *what* Benno stole, nor what I'm looking for,' Tania almost wailed.

'Nor, at a guess, do you really want to accuse Vicente. Which is wise of you.'

'*Wise?*'

'Wise, if you value your marriage, and I think you do. He sprang his proposal on you by, I admit, an unfair trick on me. But I don't believe for an instant that you accepted him simply for revenge. I think your subconscious wanted him then, and your conscious wants him still, in every way which marriage means; you must know by now that it works for you. For both of you. And that is why you will not run to him with doubts and accusations that he could very well throw back in your face. You agree?'

For you both. How little he knew about Vicente! But about herself—'You're saying I've begun to— love him?' she questioned slowly.

'My sweet girl, I could have told you so very soon after I came back to Venice! Your reluctance to admit you could ever leave him; your obedience to him about not seeing me—do you suppose I shouldn't have made violent love to you that night in Sophia's apartment, if I'd thought there was any chance of your leaving him for me?' Pascale exploded.

Her long-drawn sigh must have told him he was right, for he nodded. 'And so—no accusations?

Your marriage goes on as it has until now, and you wait?'

She managed a wan smile for him. 'You are good, Pascale. Very well—I wait.'

'And however Vicente came by it, you will enjoy his success with him?'

'I'll try——'

'Good girl!' He bent to kiss her cheek.

She was to keep the reassurance of his kiss and his parting, 'I'll keep in touch', until, near the end of a very long day on the stand, being sociable, being informative, being congratulated, a note was brought to her by hand.

It was from Pascale, saying:

'I didn't tell you this morning, as I didn't want to upset you further, but I am to go abroad again immediately after the close of the Fair. I am to be a kind of ambassador for Vetro Mestiere, with teams of salesmen under me. I do not know how long I shall be away, but this time I shall have settled addresses, and I meant it when I said I would keep in touch. For I will, and hope you will let me have news of you. I am sure you know what I feel for you, Tania, though perhaps not how hard it has been to resist persuading you into my arms. It is for that reason that I would rather not see you again before I go. But don't forget me, please.'

Tania read it through twice, tears of self-pity starting to her eyes. He could do no more for her, and it was best that they should not meet again. But she had never felt so alone in her life.

CHAPTER TEN

THE wild weather continued to batter the city, and it was on the darkest morning yet that Tania woke . . . knowing.

Nothing of physical discomfort nor mental apprehension had roused her; nothing but that flash of intuitive certainty which *knew* undeniably that she was pregnant. She hadn't been dreaming; she was very wide awake, but for moments the conviction seemed to be all her mind contained. But as coherent thought took over, she was remembering and noticing signs and odd disturbances which she had ignored at the time—her faint at the door of the *salotto*, a turn of giddiness when she had been reaching for a peach, and Vicente's question on the night she had fainted—'Is there anything you want to tell me?'—a question she had utterly misunderstood and hadn't been able to answer, but which his own intuition might have prompted, though he hadn't put it again.

Thought ranged back further still—to the night when he had taken her out on the lagoon and afterwards they had shared uninhibited love-making, as naturally inspired of their spirits' questing as that of their bodies. She remembered her hopes and her prayers of that dawn—and the despairs which had followed. But the hopes had been answered, she was as sure of it as if it were already medically confirmed. She was bearing Vicente's child, and he would have to know that in this at least she would be redeeming the debt he claimed she owed him.

All that morning she moved about in a kind of wonder. In the afternoon, when Fabia had gone to her siesta, she answered the telephone to Vicente, ringing from the foundry on San Paolo island.

'Tania? I want you to come out here. Take Rietti to Roma, where Matteo will meet you with the launch in half an hour from now. Don't keep Rietti; send him back. I shall bring you home,' he said. And to Tania's murmur of surprise—he had never asked her out to the island before—'Yes, I know the weather is bad, but you will be safe with Matteo, and it is important that you come.' He rang off without waiting for any demur or question.

Though she faced whatever he wanted her for with a nervous dread, it gave the day some purpose to call Rietti at his rooms over the garage and to get into boots and weather coat and storm hood, after leaving a message for Fabia to say where she had gone.

Matteo, Vicente's mechanic and boatman, was waiting for her at the quay, and was ready to assure her in colourful Italian that the lagoon, whether at dead calm or at full flood, was all the same to him—'As safe as God rocks me in my own bed', was the comparison he invited Tania to believe.

San Paolo was a small lone island, distant by several miles from the Murano archipelago which housed most of the other glass foundries. On San Paolo there was room only for the stark Crystos building and a hamlet of a few shops and the glass workers' cottages. Flood water lashed angrily in and around the stanchions of the boat stage as Matteo helped Tania from the launch and tied up beside one of the city's water-taxis with its pilot at the wheel.

The two men hailed each other and began to chat as Tania made her way to the main door, but before she reached it Vicente came out and drew her into the shelter of the wide porch to wait there while he went down the stage and spoke briefly to both men. He came back, windblown and wet from the teeming rain, and took Tania into the hall, where he helped her out of her coat, watched as she dropped her hood and smoothed her hair, and said, 'I shouldn't have brought you out in such conditions if it weren't important. However, you are not the only one to have braved them— we, that is, I—have a visitor, whom it is essential that you see too. Come in.'

He opened the door to his office and stood back. Benno had brought her out to the island to show her round the foundry, and she remembered the room as lacking the elegance of its counterpart in the Piazza San Marco premises, but as being a rather comfortable masculine den, with its functional desk and files offset by deep leather chairs and a divan, flanked by a drinks cabinet and a jardiniere of flowering plants.

Today, as she went in ahead of Vicente, she was aware of a figure with its back to her at the window, but only when it whirled about did she recognise Sophia Greniere.

Important? Essential—that she should be summoned here to meet her enemy? Could Vicente have devised any more cruelly bizarre a way of admitting to her the fact of his affair with Sophia than to bring them face to face here with, presumably, himself as their disputed prey? Cold with anger, she was about to demand that if he wanted a separation from her, what was wrong with a solicitor's office, when she was forestalled by Sophia's sweeping over to the desk to beat an imperious tattoo upon its surface.

'This is too much!' Sophia breathed. 'I'm leaving!' Without a second glance at Tania she began to tie a scarf over her hair and reached for a waterproof, from which, however, Vicente, going to her, disengaged her talon-like grasp, finger by finger. He flung it back over the chair from which she had taken it.

'On the contrary, you're staying,' he told her in a ice-splintering tone which Tania knew herself only too well.

'I'm going! You want to shame me. You've tricked me. But you can't keep me against my will—my man is waiting for me!'

'Not any longer, I'm afraid.'

'What do you mean? I *told* him I should need him to take me back——'

'And I've reversed the order.'

'Nonsense. How could you, since I gave it to him?'

'When I brought Tania in. Look for yourself—no, not from that window, the other—and you'll see only my launch there.' As she turned to look and then to glare again, he went on with dangerous calm, 'You invited yourself, and I haven't finished with you. When I'm ready to let you go and not before, my own launchman will see you safely home.'

She tried a last defiance. 'Your workpeople all have boats. One of them will take me!'

Vicente's glance was pitying. 'My dear, it's All Saints' Day—a working holiday, as you know. You were lucky to find me here, after tracking me everywhere more likely. But I doubt if anyone else on San Paolo would be willing to put out across the lagoon in such conditions. So forget that you're going anywhere except, before too long, safely back with Matteo,' he advised.

Between Sophia's acrimony and Vicente's steely response, Tania felt herself ignored until he pointed her to a chair which she took, supposing that sooner or later she would learn what was going on.

He continued to speak to Sophia. 'You'll understand, of course, that I sent for Tania so that she could hear from source all that it has taken me far too many weeks to force you to admit? So tell her, will you—and from the beginning, please.'

'You've wormed it out of me—isn't that enough?' Sophia flung herself petulantly into an armchair.

Vicente shook his head. 'I am not going to play reporter. You will tell her yourself that you and Benno were lovers—that he was keeping you as his mistress until the day he was killed. Begin from there.'

'Pff!' Sophia scorned. 'She knows that already.'

'From whom? From Benno?'

'Of course not from Benno, you fool! I told her myself. Or at least I let her guess.'

'Yes, so you've said. Why?'

'To put her in her place.' Sophia's glance at Tania was pure venom. 'She thought she had got Benno for love, and how we were both laughing! And then she got *you*, though I don't know how or why.'

'And you're not being told. But go on—Tell Tania why you and Benno were laughing?'

'Because his marrying her wasn't going to make any difference to *us*. He was only doing it to get hold of some valuable trade secret of her father's, which she knew nothing about. In fact, before he was killed he already had charge of the papers about it, and was offering it around for sale, and counted on its making a fortune, though you, he said, had been blind enough to turn it down.'

Tania's hands, so far idle in her lap, turned into each other, knuckles tautly white, nails digging into her palms. So far she understood and even knew the story. But something here was wrong. She remembered Benno's telling Pascale that Vicente's interest in his discovery had been lacklustre, but Vicente must have changed his mind. For he had *used* the idea. The painted crystal at the Fair was the result!

She was mystified even further when she heard Vicente tell Sophia, 'Because it was of no commercial interest to us. Crystos has no need to woo the middle market when it commands the prestige it does with quality crystal. I had no intention of lowering our standards to embrace a cheap line in machine engraving. But go on—tell Tania what happened to Reggio Morre's plans for inexpensive glass which Benno—like the word or not—stole?'

Sophia shrugged. 'You've made me tell you. *You* can tell her.'

'Very well.' Vicente turned to Tania. 'When I dealt with Benno's effects after his death, I found nothing at all pertaining to an idea of your father's for attracting the mass market in glass which he, Benno, had sketched out to me and which I had turned down.'

Tania said faintly, 'I know. When I asked you about the papers I'd let Benno deal with, you said you'd found nothing of interest to me.'

'Exactly. And I had to extract from our friend Sophia here that, knowing he couldn't interest Venice under the Massimo name, he was trying his luck with the price-cutting markets behind the Iron Curtain, passing off the plans as his own after destroying the evidence of their origin with your father.'

Tania was fighting through a maze of bewilderment. 'So that——?' she began, and stopped.

'So that—what?' Vicente echoed.

'Nothing.' Not for worlds would she admit to her doubts of him in front of Sophia. He had stolen nothing! The revolutionary painted crystal owed nothing to her father! He knew Benno had cheated her and why, and he was treating Sophia as their joint enemy, ranging himself on her side. To realise it was to emerge into light from a long dark tunnel, and she could afford to wait to escape from the web of mystery and intrigue which had betrayed her to a distrust and revenge he hadn't earned.

Sophia was waxing shrill now, taunting him, 'Extract? Is that your word for—for *tricking* me into telling you all about my affair with Benno? When it began, how long it lasted—which it did until the night he was killed, speeding to keep a date with me, and would have gone on after she'— a vindictive finger pointed at Tania—'was married to him. *Tricking* me into letting me think you had fallen for me, when all you wanted was to "extract"—*gouge* out of me all I knew about Benno's wheeling and dealing and whether or not he was unfaithful to *her*. Well, he was and was going to be, and if you've given her a few bad nights over your affair with me, I'm glad. Do you hear, *glad*! For she's the jealous sort who will take some convincing. If, that is, she ever had anything but designs upon you as the Massimo

who didn't get away . . . And what's more'—she
reached again for her coat and this time Vicente
did not interfere—'you still don't know the truth
about her and Pascale Fedore, do you? Oh yes,
she was ready to drop him when she got you instead. But since? Well, no doubt you will be
asking her and doing your best to believe her. So
may I wish you joy of whatever you make of her
lies?'

'You may,' said Vicente tautly, 'wish me joy of
anything you like, as long as this is the last either
Tania or I or Venice itself need see of you in the
future.'

'And you can count on that,' Sophia declared
vehemently. 'I can't wait to get out of this—this
mouldering *sink* of a city——'

'Back to join your husband again, perhaps?'

She glared at him. 'That's no business of
yours!'

'Nor is it,' he agreed blandly. 'When it happens,
it is going to be Signor Greniere's own.' He stood
up. 'Do I take it you are ready now for Matteo to
take you home?'

'Of course.'

'Then I'll escort you to the launch and tell him
he must come back for us.'

Without another glance at Tania she swept out
ahead of him and the door closed behind them.

Left alone, Tania faced near-panic. Vicente
could not be long away, and what was she to say
to him; what had he to say to her? There would
be questions, things they both needed to know

and tell, and Sophia had left enough poison behind to make her dread her side of the telling. When he came back, which of them would speak first to the other? There was so much to say, and so pitifully little past experience of how to say it.

She had gone to the window to watch the launch away, but she had turned to face the door when he came back. He stood there for a moment, then in a spontaneous invitation he had never made her before he opened his arms wide to her. Wondering, her eyes searching his grave beloved face, she moved a hesitant step or two, then ran abandonedly to him. His arms closed about her and he said to her head, bent to his breast, 'You have a great deal to tell me, *carissima*, have you not?'

She looked up. 'And you——? To tell me?'

'Both of us. Too much that should have been said and wasn't a long time ago.' He led her to the divan and sat beside her, turned to her, her hands held in his. 'But thank God it's not too late for some of the questions and answers now, and even if some remain, we have all time before us. Tell me, you knew about that woman and Benno, she says. How, and for how long?'

'Since the day I tried to leave the Villa and you refused to let me go. Since the day he was killed, going to meet her, and I knew he was, because I had overheard him say so on the telephone to someone he called Pascale——'

'Fedore. You didn't know him at that time?'

'No. Just the name. I gathered they were

friends who hadn't met recently, because Benno had to tell him about me and about how he was only marrying me for—for——' Tania broke off. 'Oh, it was horrible!'

Vicente prompted, 'But you remembered it all. Go on.'

She went on, reciting the ugliness for him as she had done to fill in Pascale's memory of it. She watched Vicente's frown lines deepen and his mouth set before he demanded harshly, 'Why didn't you tell me all this that night?'

She took her hand out of his and pressed her fingers to her temple. 'Because you—you'd already judged me. And you were so distant and unfeeling that I *couldn't* plead with you to believe me.'

He retorted, 'And on the evidence which you let me read, do you suppose I had many warm feelings to spare from mourning a brother and from comforting Madrigna who had loved him far more than he deserved of her?' Throwing back his shoulders and sighing, '*I* knew Benno for what he was, a lightweight, woman-crazy, vain, spendthrift to a degree—but he had conned us both into thinking he was deeply in love with you, and because in that I saw his salvation, I could have cursed you—yes, *cursed* you for breaking with him as I thought you had. Even though already you had begun to work some magic of attraction for me too,' he finished.

Tania protested, 'Oh no! You hated me!'

'Against my will, hated and loved you at the

same time. It can happen.'

'I—know.'

He glanced at her. 'You too?'

'Not then. You'—she sought a word—'loomed over my life. You had a dreadful fascination for me, but I despised myself for—for melting when you made love to me, and *wanted* to hate you.'

'Then why didn't you tell me later how I had wronged you? Why didn't you leave and go back to England?'

'At first, because you made staying my duty to Madrigna, and I couldn't hurt her with the truth about Benno. Then later, when I thought you were in his plot to cheat me and my father, I wanted my revenge. And later still, when I had begun to love you, I was jealous of Sophia. Whatever you had done, I didn't want revenge any more. I wanted *you!*'

'You didn't let me know it,' he reproached.

'I thought I could. I thought I had. Do you remember——?'

'The night I took you out on the lagoon and round the islands? Yes, very well.' Their eyes met, full of meaning; then both looked away and Tania hurried on,

'But then you listened to Sophia's lies about my meeting Pascale in her apartment, and when I couldn't deny that I had, you left me, ignored me, abandoned me in every way of marriage, and that'—her voice shook—'that is going on still.'

'Not any more, my lovely one. Why do you think I sent for you today? Because you had let

me see you were jealous of Sophia, and I wanted
to show you at first hand on just what terms she
and I really were.'

'You have been seeing a lot of her, and I saw
you take her in your arms at the Padua *festa*.'

His rare smile came and went. 'Not for the only
time, I confess. There is only one language the
Sophias of this world understand, and I used it to
get where I wanted, and ultimately did.'

'Where you wanted?' Tania echoed.

'Yes. I had already heard of her reputation—a
grass widow, only waiting to divorce until she saw
the chance of a better meal ticket—and she was
suspect from the moment she came to the Villa,
claiming Benno as a "mere friend". If "friends"
was all they had been, why hadn't the association
dropped at his death? And if they had been more,
why had Benno never brought her to the Villa,
and why hadn't she made herself known to us at
his funeral, I argued. Or called upon Madrigna
since? And when she invited herself through you
and began to flaunt herself at me, I decided to
cultivate her in order to find out just what she
and Benno had been to each other. And rather
particularly, to find out whether she knew what
he had done with your father's plans after I had
turned them down——'

At a little whisper of sound from Tania Vicente
checked. 'What?' he asked.

'Just that I had the same idea. *I* wanted to know
her, to see what she could tell me about them. I
meant to quiz her the night she tricked me into

meeting Pascale alone in her apartment. She wasn't there, and very soon afterwards she made it very clear we were enemies. So I got no further than I did with Pascale, whom I encouraged for the same reason.'

Vicente smiled again. 'I did better with Sophia—by dangling just out of her reach the carrot of her hope that I would make her my mistress. I learned how long she had been "seduced"—her word!—by Benno, and how she had always yearned for me from afar. And more practically for my purpose, that he had finally hawked the plans for a cheap machine-engraving method to the Czechs, though without much success, as far as she knew.'

'When he telephoned Pascale, he seemed to think they would make his fortune,' Tania pointed out.

'Possibly, though I doubt if any Iron Curtain developers have much to learn about price-cutting, in which, as I told Benno, Crystos doesn't need to be interested.' Vicente paused to muse, 'You know, you and I have been rather like two moles, tunnelling away along different channels, and failing to realise, until they bumped noses at the end, that they were on the same quest! Successfully, as it happened.'

'I wasn't successful,' she disclaimed. 'Until Pascale told me at the Fair that it was impossible, I thought Benno could have stolen the idea for the hand-painted crystal, and that you had used it, especially as all the rumours about your new line said the idea had stemmed from England.'

'Which it had not, though the last piece did fall into place in England. Not in any existent foundry—not even Reggio Morre's—but in the records of a long-disused plant in the north where a man and his wife, "in" glass in a small way in the seventeenth century had perfected the process, but then, perhaps for want of funds, had never gone on with it, nor marketed it. And the same formula worked for us, after years of experiment and failure. So that is the story so far of Cristallo Fiore. Does it satisfy the *signora* that it may make her fortune?' Vicente concluded in a pseudo-servile tone.

'Oh, Vicente!' His arm went round her and she leaned against him. 'Is it true? *Is* it really happening—that we've brought out all our skeletons and——?'

'——And ground them to dust? Yes, it's true, *cara*. Though yours should have been paraded for me long ago.'

'Yours, too,' she retorted with spirit. 'If you did love me, why did you let me go on thinking you married me only for punishment?'

'Loved you. Wanted you. Punished your desertion of Benno until I wormed the truth of it from Sophia, and that has taken time.'

'Until now?'

'Not quite. As soon as I had all I wanted of her, I dropped her. She pursued me here today after combing the city for me, and it struck me as a rich opportunity to force her to confess everything to you. It was no pretty sight, was it?'

Tania shuddered. 'It was horrible! And you were cruel.'

'Not too cruel. She exploited Benno's weakness for women and money, and has soured my memory of him for a very long time. She wronged you and betrayed me into new doubts of you over Pascale Fedore, just when I had begun to realise I loved you enough to forgive what you had done to Benno; just when there seemed a chance that if we both tried, we could make a real marriage out of the ugly travesty we had.'

'That was—the night you took me out on the lagoon?' she hesitated.

He nodded. 'And took you home to make love to you without, for the first time, any backlash of contempt of you or hate. You were lovely that night, Tania—all woman and, I believed, all mine.'

'As I was. But you didn't come near me again,' she mourned.

'I couldn't, while I was working that evil hag's poison out of my system. I couldn't know you were using Fedore for much the same purpose as I was using her. But now——'

Outside the winter afternoon was darkening and in the shadowed room they could hardly see each other. But rapturous awareness had no need of eyesight as they clung, strained and caressed in a hungry quest to assure, to prove, to commit, to dedicate each to the other in a humility of pledged love.

Hands wandered, explored, were kissed—Tania's palms, Vicente's, knuckle by knuckle in a tenderness of delight not yet lit to a flame of passion.

Without words they were both pleading, '*Love me!*', '*Let me love!*' without quite daring the abandonment of all the reserves and inhibitions which had kept them apart for too long. Still on a voyage of discovery of the whole love of which their bodies' cravings would be the ultimate expression, they were gentle, a little shy of the promised adventure before them, not quite trusting their fortune.

But it was there for them, the future they would make together, and when at last they drew apart, now strangely content with a passive hand-holding, they both knew it and didn't distrust it any more. And tonight—this very night which was blotting out their day—there would be no need of questioning when their every sense would be in gift and surrender to the life force which would drive their desire to the very peak of fulfilment. Tania, conscious of the gradual calming of her heartbeat, felt it quicken again at the thought and the memory of the only other night when they had come together in something near the complete accord they were knowing now. The night when——

'Madrigna is going to be pleased.' Vicente's voice broke into the silence with a remark which was entirely off beam from her thoughts.

She adjusted with difficulty. 'About us, you mean? But isn't she reasonably happy for us already? We have never let her guess at our particular troubles, have we?'

'No. Nor ever must. Benno must remain for her the beloved figure he always was, just as we must never have been at odds. But no—I wasn't thinking of any change in her feelings towards us. I was picturing her approval of us for supplying her with a long-felt want. Do you know what I mean? Or must I remind you of an evening when you fainted on your way into dinner, and denied you had anything to tell me when I asked?'

Off beam? On beam indeed, if with that remark about Fabia's gratitude, he had been hinting he had already guessed at her secret *then*! She said, 'I do remember. But I wasn't lying when I said No. I didn't know myself that——'

'That you were pregnant with my child? That *is* what we are talking about, beloved?'

Tania nodded happily. 'Yes. But how could you have known?'

'It was only a shot in the dark then. But before that you had seemed to get more listless by the hour and when you did that faint it occurred to me it could be the answer. And it was? Is?'

'Is,' she echoed. 'But I've only known for certain since I woke this morning.'

'This morning? You have checked with Doctor Carloni?' he puzzled, and she laughed.

'No. But don't worry. I tell you I *woke* knowing it—in my very bones. So be happy for me, for us . . . for the three of us,' she begged.

Vicente's answer was to tilt her chin and to kiss her as lightly as if her lips had been brushed by a moth's wing.

'That is for a clever girl who must be handled with the most delicate care and solicitude from now on,' he said.

'Oh dear!' She wrinkled her nose at him in mock dismay. 'And to think that I'd been looking forward to some full-bodied ravishment from time to time!' she teased boldly.

He took his cue. 'And have you not enjoyed ravishment at my hands already, *signora*?' he admonished.

She lowered her eyes modestly. 'Yes indeed. The *signore* has been—most attentive— But——'

'Shameless wench, are you tempting me? If so, then by heaven I'll——!' With a lascivious leer Vicente made a theatrical lunge at her, but checked and laughed ruefully at the intrusion of a strident siren note from the lagoon.

'Matteo returned for us—of all the inept timing! End of dramatic scene, I'm afraid, *signora*!' Drawing her to her feet, he held her close to whisper, 'Seriously, ravishment and my body's worship of yours postponed, *carissima*. But there are going to be many times for us—very soon.'

He fetched her coat, nestled her into it and into her hood as if she were an infinitely precious parcel, and hand-in-hand they went out and down the jetty to meet the promise to them and their city of a fallen wind, calming waters and a moon riding high.

Vicente told Matteo, 'I'll take the wheel, and my wife will sit beside me.'

My wife. To Tania's ears the ordinary phrase made the sweetest sound in the world as, under the hands she loved, the launch swept out from shore in a wide arc, leaving a curve of silver wake behind.

Three great Doctor Nurse Romances to look out for this month

There are now three Doctor Nurse Romances for you to look out for and enjoy every month. These are the titles for August

CHATEAU NURSE
by Jan Haye

After an attack of pneumonia, Nurse Hilary Hope jumps at the chance of doing some private nursing in France but does not expect her life to be turned upside down by the local devastating doctor there, Raoul de la Rue ...

HOSPITAL IN THE MOUNTAINS
by Jean Evans

After a terrible car accident, Nurse Jill Sinclair accompanies her injured brother to an Austrian clinic where Baron von Reimer hopes to repair his injuries. But the Doctor Baron is such an attractive man that Jill soon finds herself in an impossible situation ...

OVER THE GREEN MASK
by Lisa Cooper

An exciting new part of her life begins when Nurse Jennifer Turner first reports at the Princess Beatrice Hospital — but nothing works out as she'd dreamed after she meets handsome registrar, Nicholas Smythe.

On sale where you buy Mills & Boon romances

The Mills & Boon rose is the rose of romance

The Mills & Boon Rose is the Rose of Romance

Every month there are ten new titles to choose from — ten new stories about people falling in love, people you want to read about, people in exciting, far-away places. Choose Mills & Boon. It's your way of relaxing:

August's titles are:

COLLISION by *Margaret Pargeter*
After the heartless way Max Heger had treated her, Selena wanted to be revenged on him. But things didn't work out as she had planned.

DARK REMEMBRANCE by *Daphne Clair*
Could Raina marry Logan Thorne a year after her husband Perry's death, when she knew that Perry would always come first with her?

AN APPLE FROM EVE by *Betty Neels*
Doctor Tane van Diederijk and his fiancée were always cropping up in Euphemia's life. If only she could see the back of both of them?

COPPER LAKE by *Kay Thorpe*
Everything was conspiring to get Toni engaged to Sean. But she was in love with his brother Rafe — who had the worst possible opinion of her!

INVISIBLE WIFE by *Jane Arbor*
Vicente Massimo blamed Tania for his brother's death. So how was it that Tania soon found herself blackmailed into marrying him?

BACHELOR'S WIFE by *Jessica Steele*
Penny's marriage to Nash Devereux had been a ' paper ' one. So why did Nash want a reconciliation just when Penny wanted to marry Trevor?

CASTLE IN SPAIN by *Margaret Rome*
Did Birdie love the lordly Vulcan, Conde de la Conquista de Retz — who wanted to marry her — or did she fear him?

KING OF CULLA by *Sally Wentworth*
After the death of her sister, Marnie wanted to be left alone. But the forceful Ewan McNeill didn't seem to get the message!

ALWAYS THE BOSS by *Victoria Gordon*
The formidable Conan Garth was wrong in every opinion he held of Dinah — but could she ever make him see it?

CONFIRMED BACHELOR by *Roberta Leigh*
Bradley Dexter was everything Robyn disliked. But now that she could give him a well-deserved lesson, fate was playing tricks on her!

If you have difficulty in obtaining any of these books from your local paperback retailer, write to:

Mills & Boon Reader Service
P.O. Box 236, Thornton Road, Croydon, Surrey, CR9 3RU.
Available August 1981

ROMANCE

Variety is the spice of romance

Each month, Mills & Boon publish new romances. New stories about people falling in love. A world of variety in romance – from the best writers in the romantic world. Choose from these titles in September.

THE LION OF LA ROCHE   Yvonne Whittal
SATAN'S MASTER   Carole Mortimer
ILLUSION   . Charlotte Lamb
SUBSTITUTE BRIDE   Margaret Pargeter
UNTOUCHED WIFE   Rachel Lindsay
INNOCENT OBSESSION   Anne Mather
WITCHING HOUR   Sara Craven
HILLS OF AMETHYST   Mary Moore
PASSIONATE STRANGER   Flora Kidd
MACLEAN'S WOMAN   Ann Cooper

On sale where you buy paperbacks. If you require further information or have any difficulty obtaining them, write to: Mills & Boon Reader Service, PO Box 236, Thornton Road, Croydon, Surrey CR9 3RU. England.

Mills & Boon
the rose of romance

SAVE TIME, TROUBLE & MONEY!
By joining the exciting NEW...

WITH all these **EXCLUSIVE BENEFITS** for every member

NOTHING TO PAY! MEMBERSHIP IS FREE TO REGULAR READERS!

IMAGINE the *pleasure* and *security* of having ALL your favourite *Mills & Boon* romantic fiction delivered right to *your* home, absolutely POST FREE... straight off the press! No waiting! No more disappointments! All this PLUS all the latest news of *new books* and *top-selling authors* in your own monthly MAGAZINE... PLUS *regular* big CASH SAVINGS... PLUS lots of wonderful strictly-limited, *members-only* SPECIAL OFFERS! All these exclusive benefits can be *yours* – right NOW – simply by joining the exciting NEW *Mills & Boon* ROMANCE CLUB. Complete and post the coupon below for FREE full-colour leaflet. It costs nothing. HURRY!

No obligation to join unless you wish!

FREE CLUB MAGAZINE Packed with *advance* news of latest titles and authors

Exciting offers of **FREE BOOKS** For club members ONLY

Lots of fabulous **BARGAIN OFFERS** —many at **BIG CASH SAVINGS**

FREE FULL-COLOUR LEAFLET!
CUT OUT CUT OUT COUPON BELOW AND POST IT TODAY!

To: **MILLS & BOON READER SERVICE, P.O. Box No 236, Thornton Road, Croydon, Surrey CR9 3RU, England.** WITHOUT OBLIGATION to join, please send me FREE details of the exciting NEW Mills & Boon ROMANCE CLUB and of all the exclusive benefits of membership.

Please write in BLOCK LETTERS below

NAME (Mrs/Miss) ....

ADDRESS..

CITY/TOWN ....

COUNTY/COUNTRY..................... POST/ZIP CODE.............

Readers in South Africa and Zimbabwe please write to: **P.O. BOX 1872, Johannesburg, 2000. S. Africa**